Werewolf Watching

In Michigan's Upper Peninsula

A Field Guide

Werewolf Watching

In Michigan's Upper Peninsula

A Field Guide

by

DALE R. HOFFMAN

This book is a work of fiction. Names, characters, places, and incidents are either the product of the author's imagination or are used fictitiously. Any resemblance to actual persons, businesses or events, is coincidental. It's messed up that we even have to tell you this.

Deerwood Books

drumcomic.com

Cover design by
Rob S. Furr
www.furr.ca

Cover Photographs by
April Hoffman

ISBN: 978-0-9893509-0-7
ISBN: 0-9893509-0-8

DEDICATION

For April—a werewolf lover

ACKNOWLEDGMENTS

Thanks to the following for making this book possible: God, April, Harol Marshall, Deerwood Books, Jerry Meisner, and Two long-ass winters.

#	CHAPTER TITLE	PG

WOLFWORD

Congratulations! Werewolf watching has aroused your curiosity and now you are on the brink of the most exciting outdoor adventure of your lifetime. Over the following pages you will become an expert on the latest cross between science and extreme sports: werewolf watching.

How often have you encountered a rare creature on a walk in the woodlands and stood motionless in an effort to figure out what it was doing, whether it was stalking prey, and if so, who was it eating and how? Bent over with its head down, arms and legs in its mouth, perhaps? Have you paused to consider who it ate, if say, someone you know disappeared in the area? Or how it survived on a cold winter night, or how it reproduced or what it would do if it caught sight of you staring at it?

While there are excellent field guides available to help identify woodland inhabitants, none provide comprehensive information on the subject of werewolves— who they are, what they look like, what they do and why. This field guide takes up where the others leave off, providing the who, what, when, where, and why of werewolves and their native habitat. As you become familiar with the pocket guide's format, you will find that it also serves as a protector against stray bullets, especially if carried in your left breast pocket.

I have attempted in this small, low-priced volume to compress the information that otherwise can be found only on the web or in a library of horror DVDs on the subject. At some point you may be able to access all that information on your iPhone, but until then, this guide will provide a readily accessible reference source when touring the forests and trails of Michigan's unique Upper Peninsula.

About Werewolf Watching

Werewolves are shape-shifting humans who have been infected with a terrible disease: lycanthropy—the disease of werewolfism. Symptoms of werewolfism include: abundant hair, howling at the moon, changing into a raging beast, chronic gas, and ripping out someone's throat.

Werewolf watchers are enthusiasts who watch these bloodthirsty beasts. They are people who have the desire to accomplish a level of recreational danger not seen by many people, except for a few short moments before their own deaths.

Today's werewolf watchers enjoy a more accelerated lifestyle than most wildlife enthusiasts like bird watchers. That's because spotting a purple finch in your driveway isn't half as exciting as learning that a close relative is a bloodthirsty werewolf.

Now that's one to tell the grandkids about, if you live. Excitement? You bet!

Excitement is why werewolf watching is becoming one of the fastest growing recreational activities in North America. Not *the* fastest growing activity, but *becoming* the fastest growing. In other words, even though it isn't the fastest growing recreational activity, we are approaching a time where it may grow, maybe even becoming the fastest.

The best part about werewolf watching is that anyone can do it, young or old, rich or poor. Like any other sport, all it takes is a little patience, experience, and tens of thousands of dollars worth of specialized equipment from various sporting supply stores. For those on a tighter budget, homemade equipment can be made with duct tape.

The level of available fun is up to each and every werewolf watcher who ventures out to take their chances. Throughout this book, you will learn the proper equipment, techniques, tactics and methods of the werewolfing community. Once you are experienced, it's up to you, the individual werewolfer, to put your own skills to the test.

The Science of Werewolf Watching

Werewolf watching is called Wolfithology, not to be confused with Lycanthology, the study of werewolves. We've all seen Lycanthologists in the movies—some old priest pouring over ancient texts in the monastery library. He studies werewolves by candlelight and by the time he decides to kill one, boom, he's dead.

Wolfithology is not passive, nor is it a deliberate act of hunting. It's a twenty-first century extreme sport: the practice of watching a dangerous supernatural beast that will probably eat your throat, as it exists in its own natural habitat. But don't be intimidated by the scientific terminology.

In common usage, werewolf watching is called werewolfing and those who do the werewolfing are referred to as werewolfers. These are the terms the worldwide werewolfing community uses. Remember, werewolfing can be enjoyed by everyone—wealthy and poor, smart and dumb, children and the elderly. Also, werewolves eat many of these people.

Werewolves are found throughout North America, but this book is dedicated to werewolfing in Michigan's Upper Peninsula. The U.P. is a unique territory where climate, geography, and an ancient Scandinavian bloodline all combine to create almost perfect werewolfing. In recent decades, werewolf populations in the U.P. have almost tripled. Although scientists have yet to return my calls, the werewolfing community has managed to compile much data.

After you begin werewolfing, if you are interested in submitting your data, please visit the website:

www.where'smylefthand.com.

Enter your data on the chart provided and remember that all reports are 100 percent anonymous. Enter your name, address, phone number, email, social security number and bank routing number in the spaces provided.

Werewolfing Tips

Before you begin werewolfing, there are some key points we need to cover in order to ensure your success. Physical risks like blisters and calluses exist in almost any wilderness adventure. In this case we'll be risking blisters, calluses and a horrible death by carnivorous mutilation as well.

To avoid this fate, you must adhere to a set standard of practical rules. If you follow procedures, and procure the proper equipment, there is no reason you can't become as proficient a werewolfer as any of the top advocates in the world, like Dr. Straus Hienlenkof, one of the top five international werewolfers last seen staking out a werewolf somewhere near Atlantic Mine, MI.

Other famous werewolfers include Ross Trengle, Eileen Skarzy, and Tom

Whiting, known as *The Werewolf Three*, last seen south of Ishpeming, MI, except for Mr. Trengle who returned from the excursion but was later shot for being a werewolf. With a little hard work and patience, you too can reap the rewards as they have. GOOD LUCK!

Dale R. Hoffman
Author, and enthusiast

CHAPTER 1
THE FIRST U.P. WEREWOLF

Although Europeans began arriving in America centuries before, it wasn't until 1838 that the bloodline of the Lycanthrope arrived in the U.P. from Scandinavia. During that period, copper was discovered in Michigan's Upper Peninsula resulting in a mining boom that was bigger than the California Gold Rush. The influx of Scandinavians brought with them highly skilled mining techniques that were desperately needed to haul ore out of the ground. They also brought the ancient curse of werewolfism, something that wasn't desperately needed at the time. You could even say it was frowned upon.

The 16th century Swedish writer Olaus Magnus wrote that the Livonian werewolves were initiated by draining werewolf blood into a cup of someone's beer and repeating a set formula. It was through a love of beer that the first U.P. werewolf was formed.

The first known Upper Peninsula Werewolf was a Finn named Eito Elchick. In the summer of 1837, Eito lived in Slrjk, Finland. Although most of his friends and family were miners, Eito felt that manure farming was the future. One day, Eito said, "It's 1837 and everyone needs manure for one reason or another—crops for example, or maybe just for farting around."

Eito fed his cattle everyday and became known for his excessive piles of bull-crap. People would come from miles away just to get a whiff.

Some would ask, "What's that stink?"

Others would reply, "That's Eito's bull-crap."

Aside from great piles of crap, Eito had some bad habits. He could often be seen cruising various alehouses in Scandinavia sneaking beer from unattended mugs of patrons. As soon as someone would turn their back, Eito would guzzle their beer and sneak away. The Finns had a term for this sort of person—"Viina Haukka," or "Booze-hawk."

During the soccer season of 1838, the Finnish soccer team defeated Sweden in an exciting one-nil victory that could only be described as the most boring sporting event in recorded history. After ninety minutes of play, the game remained tied at 0-0.

This was long before The World Cup, and in those days when a tie occurred, instead of having an overtime period, the two teams would engage in a drinking competition at midfield. White oak kegs of ale were rolled out and tapped. When only one person was left standing, victory was declared one to nil.

The Finns achieved this victory when Artten Slaupphalaa funneled a flagon of

Nordic ale, sending his only remaining Swedish competitor, Slorji Yorji, to the turf. All of Finland erupted in celebration and every "Great Hall" in Scandinavia, even in Sweden, began a week long festival of guzzling ale and eating boiled goats, boiled fish, boiled potatoes, and random things that were boiled just for the heck of it.

Eito was cruising through one of these great halls, stealing swallows of beer from distracted soccer fans when a shiny silver beer-mug caught his eye. Unbeknownst to Eito, the owner of the mug was a sorcerer who had concocted a special beer mixed with the blood of the Lycanthrope. He planned to give the concoction to a local magistrate who'd just issued him a citation for operating a horse-drawn cart while under the influence of ale.

In those days, sorcerers were like rock stars. Distracted by a groupie's bosoms, the sorcerer took his eye off the silver mug and Eito swooped in. He gulped the blood-laced ale and snuck away.

When the sorcerer turned around and noticed the empty mug he said, "Hey! Who's the booze-hawk?" But Eito was gone, already drinking someone else's beer.

Later that night, Eito fell ill. He became too sick to work. Weeks went by. He didn't have his usual booze-hawk energy and his manure farm went to crap. One night around sunset, there came a knock on Eito's door. Eito pulled himself out of his bed and managed to open it. It was his creditors, a group of local businessmen that Eito failed to pay when his manure farm started going down the crapper.

"Hey Eito," they said. "You owe us some cash you sack of manure."

"I'm sick. Something is wrong with me. I haven't been able to farm manure."

"That's because you're always drinking beer from other people's glasses."

Eito threw up on his creditors.

"We'll be back in two weeks, Eito, and you better have our money or we're going to make manure out of you."

The disgruntled businessmen left as the sun began to set over the hills and the full moon began to rise. Eito began to itch all over his body. *Oh no,* he thought, *a rash.* He raised his gaze to the heavens. "Dear God, if you make me better, I promise I'll never booze-hawk anyone again."

No dice.

The fur began to sprout; his bones creaked and stretched and he writhed around on the floor screaming. Right when the pain became unbearable he noticed something under the kitchen table.

"Hey," he said. "There's those fingernail clippers I was looking for the other day."

He tried to grab them, but the metamorphosis continued. Long wolf nails popped out of his fingertips and he thought to himself, isn't that ironic? *I finally found the clippers and now my nails are too long to clip!*

His body changed faster and faster. His limbs stretched, and razor sharp teeth popped out of his gums. Eito thought to himself, that was some crappy beer.

The full moon was high above the manure farm. The front door of Eito's manure shack burst open and a werewolf named Eito Elchick emerged, howling a high-pitched yelp that was not even remotely terrifying. It was pathetic, like someone had slammed a door on his finger. He ran towards town on all fours yelping and bumping his rear-end on the ground. His new werewolf nose could only smell the scent of blood, and of course, the residual manure from the farm.

Months went by. People began to disappear. Eito's manure farm went down the toilet and the townsfolk were afraid to talk to him. Eito's creditors sent him a letter via donkey that he was to vacate the premise immediately, so on the night of the full moon Eito headed downtown. The alehouses were emptying out except for a few stragglers who were too drunk to get up. Eito hid in some bushes waiting for passers by, and as luck would have it one of his creditors, Willjjeerr Aho, came staggering down the street toting a full mug of ale.

Eito followed him for a while, tip-toeing on furry Finlander werewolf feet. One time Willjjeerr thought he heard something behind him, but convinced himself it was nothing, sort of like people do in horror movies.

Eito kept following and ducking into the bushes, keeping out of sight. When they were out of view from town, he struck! He leapt at Willjjeerr's throat, but missed and hit the ground like a ton of bricks.

"What the . . . " said Willjjeerr.

"I've got your credit right here," said Eito and he lunged again, this time grabbing the ale out of Willjjeerr's hand and guzzling it.

"What kind of wolf are you?" said Willjjeerr.

"Sorry, old habits die hard," growled Eito.

"Eito, is that you?"

"How could you tell?"

"Because you drank my beer and you smell like manure."

"Doesn't matter, Wiljjeerr, I'm gonna rip your throat out!"

"Bring it on, fuzzball. I'm gonna take that credit you owe me right out of your furry little keaster!"

But it was too late. Eito was on top of him, his five-foot-eight, one-hundred-thirty-pound frame struggling to overpower the two-hundred-pound drunken Willjjeerr.

After staggering around in a circle with Eito on top of his head, Willjjeerr tripped over a stump, fell and hit his head on a stone, killing him.

"Yes!" growled Eito. He ate Willjjeerr's throat, washing it down with the remaining ale, and ran off into the woods, bloodied and liquored up.

The next day, Eito woke up in his manure barn. He looked at his naked body covered in blood, ale and manure. On the floor beside him was Willjjeerr's empty mug. Whoa, he thought. *Rave party! People are probably going to talk.*

No sooner had the thought entered his mind when he heard a noise in the distance drawing closer. It sounded like voices. He peeked through the wall of the manure barn and saw an angry mob with pitchforks and hoes and torches, even though it was broad daylight. I mean they were pissed!

"Eito Elchick! We're going to hang you! You killed Willjjeerr Aho last night."

How'd they know it was me? thought Eito.

"We knew it was you because whoever killed Willjjeerr stole his ale and smelled like manure."

That's how.

But the angry mob didn't know he was hiding in the barn. They went to the front door of his dung-shack. As they kicked in the door of his shack, Eito slipped out of the back of the manure barn, and escaped into the woods.

Eito walked for miles and miles through the forest. He found some pants hanging on a farmhouse clothesline. He also found a blouse but opted not to wear it. He decided he would keep walking to the seashore. There were boats down there and maybe he could stow away on one. He had to escape Finland before word got out that he was a werewolf.

Eito reached the seashore and blended in to the dockside hustle and bustle, except for the fact that he was only wearing pants. Along the docks the ships were being loaded. Inside the taverns, sailors were getting loaded. Eito wandered around the docks, lost in his hung-over werewolf fog.

"Hey Eito!" yelled a voice.

Eito turned around only to notice Dan Grrllggjjii, his old pal from Manure College.

"Dan? What the heck are you doing here?"

"We're loading up this ship to set sail for the Upper Peninsula of Michigan. You looking for work?"

"Heck yeah, I am!"

"It's hard work," said Dan. "They're mining copper."

"I don't care if they're mining muskrat turds, I gotta get out of here!"

"Okay, Eito. Meet me on that boat over there."

"Okay, Dan. I'll be there in twenty minutes. There's something I have to do."

Eito snuck into the alehouse and stole a swallow of beer from every person's mug, then met Dan on the boat. The ship set sail and Eito looked off the stern towards a shrinking Finland. As the sun began to set, he could see the glow of torches and pitchforks from his hometown angry mob. They had reached the coast and were working their way down the hill to the seashore.

I made it just in time, he thought. *And I got some free beer too.*

When the ship arrived at the Soo Locks in Michigan's Upper Peninsula, Eito was the only one left.

"Where the heck is everyone?" asked the Porter.

"Uh (burp), I don't know," said Eito. "They . . . must have fallen overboard."

"Oh well," said the Porter, "stuff happens."

Eito took to the Upper Peninsula of Michigan like gravy on a pasty, and the U.P. bloodline began.

CHAPTER 2
BEER AND WEREWOLVES

All werewolves love to drink beer, especially domestic light beer. From this point forward, Domestic Light Beer shall be referred to as (DLB).

Beer drinking and Lycanthropy have been intertwined since before recorded history. Lycanthropy is an old disease that is believed to have begun somewhere around Scandinavia and other parts of Europe where beer drinking has a long, tasty tradition.

In Scandinavia, Lycanthropy was commonly called Hunter's Disease because hunters were the first to bring it home from the woods. Lycanthropy is spread by fluid exchange from an infected werewolf to an unlucky individual through scratching, biting, unprotected sex or the sharing of dirty werewolf needles. Werewolves can also reproduce through mating with other werewolves. This is sometimes a direct result of beer drinking.

During Viking times people drank honey mead instead of beer. It was common practice for local sorcerers to spike an individual's honey mead with werewolf blood, thus infecting their intended victim with Lycanthropy. This was done out of spite.

Imagine you have a disagreement with your neighbor; say he cut down one of your trees. In Viking times, instead of going to small claims court you would find a sorcerer and pay him to spike your neighbor's mead with werewolf blood. Later on, you and several of your friends would participate in the mob killing of your neighbor because he was a werewolf.

Centuries later, during 712 A.D., Lycanthropy reached epidemic proportions. Close to a third of Scandinavia's population became furry. This culminated in a series of new nicknames that were neither clever nor appreciated.

During the Middle Ages, Lycanthropy was not fatal, but death was often the result as neighbors and townsfolk became agitated or frightened. They formed angry mobs and said things like, "We have to do the right thing here: kill this guy with pitchforks and axes while hiding anonymously behind a group of other townsfolk."

Because of mob justice, the practice of blood spiking was banned. This would later lead to the organization of the Scandinavian Sorcerer's Union (see: *Practicing Sorcery in Michigan's Upper Peninsula,* by Dale R. Hoffman), and the revival of blood spiking for a brief period during the days of Eito Elchick.

Beer Gets Better

Over the next few centuries, thanks to the meticulous calculations of monks, beer drinking evolved from honey mead to barley malt and hops.

Yeasts were cultivated instead of gathered from the wild and this resulted in much better tasting beer. Because of this new brewing method, Lycanthropy surged. In the eighteen hundreds the population boom of Europe breathed new life into werewolves.

One of the first people to notice the increasing werewolf population was a man named Oleff Kleinsausser, officially known as the first modern-day werewolfer. Kleinsausser was a goat farmer in 1837, who lived down the road from Eito Elchick.

In 1946, a soldier returning from World War II bought a small farm near where Eito lived in Finland. He shot his first deer that fall and inside the deer's stomach, he found Kleinsausser's diary still intact, which began with the following entry:

Aye, I fear for young Eito that he has come ill with the disease of ye hunter. He howls at ye moon 'round ye midnight and barks and scratches like a hound. He smells of waste, yea though he be a manure farmer and this is typical, still, he howls at ye moon and barks and scratches.

Kleinsausser kept a daily journal from the first time he noticed his neighbor acting strange. It is through this diary that we have gained many insights into the history of werewolfing, like this passage:

June 17, 1837: Eito left ye manure farm early this morn. Aye I shall follow him this eve and draw ye a picture of what he be doing.

Kleinsausser, an experienced hunter, followed Eito during the greater lunar cycles and recorded what he saw:

Aye and I can see him now, yonder of two hundred cubits in front of me. He's a wolf I tell you. The disease lives. He is so terrifying I have consumed numerous ales to better steady my nerve. With me I have brought a magnifying glass to better look at him, and ink and feather and yea I shall sketch him quickly. Although I am drunk, Eito is ferocious, drunker than I and foul with the smell of cow-droppings. Surely I must finish before he sees me...(burp)...uh-oh. Aye he heard me. Crap, I should've brought ye gun... Here he comes...ahhhh!

Today, despite the development of modern technology, only a handful of werewolfers live. The important thing is that they have managed to gain unrestricted access to their prize.

The U.P. Mining Boom

Making his way to Michigan to join the Upper Peninsula mining boom of the 1840s, Eito Elchick managed to attack enough people to maintain the healthy population of werewolves that exist today. This rise in population coincided with constant improvements in the consistency and alcohol content of DLB.

As miners pulled more and more copper ore from the mines, they consumed more and more beer, creating more and more werewolves. These new werewolf-miners developed a love affair with light pilsner-style lagers, most commonly brewed in places like St. Louis, Milwaukee, Chicago and Colorado, but it was the local breweries of the U.P. that fueled modern werewolfing.

The 1980s gave rise to the micro-brew revolution. No longer did werewolves have to drink cheap pilsner-style lagers. Beers such as Sam Adams, Sierra Nevada Pale ale and especially Pete's Wicked Ale (brewed by actual werewolves) offered the werewolfing public the flavor of the old country at a lower price than imports. This opened up the werewolfing economy significantly, and great werewolf watchers sprung up all over the U.P, like Merna Shlauski, last seen near L'anse Michigan.

Today, as the economy has tightened, werewolves have tightened their beer budgets. This has lead to a throwback popularity of cheap pilsner beers such as

Busch Light, Old Style, Black Label, and god forbid, The Silver Bullet. The rule is as follows: the cheaper the DLB someone is drinking, the greater the likelihood they are a werewolf.

DLB has become one of the best tools we have today for the observation of Upper Peninsula werewolves. Studies are showing, we believe, that today's U.P. werewolves are tipsier than ever. If someone in your family or perhaps one of your neighbors consumes excessive amounts of these types of beers, it is possible they are infected with Lycanthropy. However, this may not be the case, as these types of beers are still popular with locals.

CHAPTER 3
GETTING STARTED

Before you head into the backcountry of the Upper Peninsula, it is critical to acquire the skills and tools of the seasoned werewolfer. A checklist should be compiled so that nothing is left to chance. Weather info, a compass, proper clothing, a six-pack, these are all factors in the success of your journey. Remember, a detail-oriented werewolfer is a werewolfer who comes home with all four limbs and his sixty cents worth of returnables.

Because the U.P. is ever changing, you may be staking out a werewolf in an urban area as well as a rural environment. Your checklist should also include a functioning speedometer in your car, a car stereo that can pick up some decent classic rock, and some coupons for Starbucks. If you don't have a Starbucks in your area, any imitation will do. Remember, it is important to stay alert when werewolfing. Also, werewolves may attack coffee drinkers.

Equipment Check

Below is a standard equipment checklist for the average Upper Peninsula excursion.

Silver Bullets

This author does not recommend shooting any werewolf on sight, as the individual may just be your neighbor or the cable guy.

Recognizing werewolves

It is important to know that werewolves may sometimes disguise themselves as your neighbor or the cable guy.

Head Gear

A jungle hat is preferred with different shades of camouflage for different seasons—wide rim for summertime sun, earflaps for wintertime wind. Also, a helmet with two beer holders and some plastic tubing that runs directly into your mouth is recommended. Spring werewolfing is not recommended as werewolves are mating and males may mistake you for a female.

Hard hats are sometimes worn by werewolfers but offer very little protection. You should have a couple of beers attached to your helmet with tubing that runs to your mouth. Dr. Klein Wilmer of Pelkie, Michigan was famous for the bright blue hardhat he wore on excursion. They found it under some leaves next to a pile of vital organs later determined to be his. No one is sure how Wilmer died. Some people think he passed out and was later eaten by coyotes. There is not enough data.

Sunglasses

Sunglasses offer great protection against the sun's harmful rays and may also make a werewolf watcher appear to be cool, even if they're a dork. Mirrored sunglasses are not recommended as you may look like the lead singer from Steppenwolf. This may attract werewolves toward you.

Goggles

Goggles are helpful when running for your life through the woods, but be advised, they offer little protection against the sun's harmful UV rays.

Torso Protection

A shark-proof chain mail shirt or a Kevlar vest that covers the torso and neck area are preferred by most seasoned werewolfers, but because of rising costs and increasing popularity of the sport, most werewolfers just put on a t-shirt and some shorts. You may be able to wear light clothing without injury for years, months, or even days.

Pants

Depending on the terrain and climate, you may need to wear some type of pants. If this is the law where you live, you may want to comply with local ordinances.

Footwear

Durable footwear is essential for just about every outdoor activity. Hard-soled shoes or boots, or footwear that allows you to run very fast are recommended. Most amateur werewolfers start out by dressing like birdwatchers, but as they become more experienced they tend to dress more like Olympic Sprinters.

Telephoto camera and lenses

If you want to get some great close-up

action-photos of werewolves, a telephoto lens is a must. If you cannot afford one, you can make your own out of duct tape.

Today, advances in photography have allowed werewolfers to compete on an equal level with wildlife photographers. Before advances in photography, werewolfers had to get very close to snap a photo. This led to an increase in Lycanthropy (the disease of werewolfism) and a decrease in the number of werewolfers (eaten).

Many modern werewolfing techniques have been developed since then, reducing casualties upwards of one-half of one percent.

Binoculars

Binoculars are fine if you simply want to go out with the kids for some Sunday afternoon werewolfing, but in the worldwide community you'll need to snap some photos. Also, before heading out you'll want to have your affairs in order.

Suit of Armor

Those Knights had it right when they surrounded their entire bodies with steel to ward off swords, spears, and monsters. If you can obtain a suit of armor you can be almost unstoppable in the world of werewolf watching. Note: suits of armor do not prevent dismemberment and may slow you down.

Modern Commercial Suits of Armor

Today there are many types of refashioned suits of armor. Stylish and comfortable, these contemporary suits feature molded plastic joint pieces and cast aluminum, which offer even less protection than iron. However, if a werewolf eats you while wearing one of these, you will look so sweetly medieval.

Chain Mail Armor

Beneath most suits of armor is a mesh

covering referred to as chain mail. These suits are used in the protection of divers from shark bites as well as in the world of butchering, to prevent people from losing fingers. Also, werewolves pick their teeth and wipe their rear ends with Chain Mail Armor.

Football/Hockey Uniforms

Football and hockey equipment is surprisingly durable when it comes to werewolf attacks. The lightweight construction makes it easier to flee from watched werewolves, but it should only be used in conjunction with a solid structure for hiding, like a creepy cabin in the woods.

As with most sports equipment, unless there is a game going on, you may look ridiculous. People may pepper you with questions like, "Where you going, Gipper?" or "Nice get up, Gordy Howe." Take comfort in the fact that they are not werewolfers and you are. How long will they be enjoying their hobbies—ten, twenty years? You'll be werewolf watching for days on end.

Shorts and T-shirts

Shorts and t-shirts are recommended for most werewolfing excursions for the simple fact that it doesn't really matter what you wear, that werewolf is going to rip the crap out of your throat if he catches you. Remember, comfort counts.

Other Equipment

Basic camping and backpacking equipment will be required for any type of extended wilderness excursion. Cold foods should be packed for your trip as cooking and campfires attract werewolves. Werewolves love to eat people and often disguise themselves as other campers or backpackers who just want to pop in for a couple of beers around the fire

This was first observed by Dr. John Walton of Chatham Michigan, a famous werewolfer last seen camping in the Hiawatha National Forest area. Walton spent his life searching for foods that werewolves loathed. He believed that if he found certain foods that werewolves had aversions to, he could release a line of werewolf repellent.

Walton's theory states: *Anchovies are disgusting, and therefore, werewolves may not like them.*

Anchovies were later found to be a favorite food of werewolves. Dr. Walton was also found to be a favorite food of werewolves.

Packing your gear

The organized werewolfer is the successful werewolfer. Pack your gear in Ziploc bags and store food in werewolf-proof containers, available at most werewolf equipment outlet stores. If you cannot afford containers, use duct tape.

It is important to pack quiet gear. Do not pack gear that will rattle around and make noise when you run for your life. Werewolves are alerted by noise and if they hear you they will run away, or towards you. Silence is the key to successful werewolfing

If there are a number of people in your party, try to keep the shrieks of terror to a minimum.

Dr. Rachael Haafla of Michigan Tech University had this to say about being quiet in the forest:

Anyone can hike into a werewolf-infested forest but the skills of the hunter, not the scientist, are required for great werewolfing. Right now, for example, I've spotted a werewolf about a hundred yards away, (achoo) ... ooh ... I think he heard me ... uh oh ... yes he heard me ...ahhhh!

It was through her extreme determination that Dr. Haafla briefly became one of the leading worldwide werewolfers, and with the help of this book, so can you! Remember, all it takes is a little blood, sweat and tears.

Now that you have your equipment, let's get werewolfing!

CHAPTER 4
THE DISEASE

Werewolfism is defined as the behavior of a werewolf. Whereas Lycanthropy is the actual disease of werewolfism, werewolfism is thought to refer to the behavior of the afflicted individual. Werewolfism is the changing of a human into a supernatural wolf-like creature to a greater degree than what is typical or proper.

It is a misconception to think werewolfism refers only to the desire to rip out throats for pleasure. In actuality, it refers to any situation where a werewolf can gain pleasure from something in excess and morphs into a carnivorous man-beast in order to do so. This includes werewolf sex, werewolf snowmobiling, computer games, cigarettes, alcohol, buying fatback and social media.

Significance

Traditionally, most religions have deemed werewolfism a deadly sin. This is made clear in many of the Proverbs. For example:

Do not join those werewolves who drink too much wine or gorge themselves on throat-ripping, for drunkards and gluttons become poor and shape-shifting clothes them in rags, even though the tailors love it.

Also:

He who keeps the law is a discerning son, but a companion of werewolves disgraces his father at least once a month.

And:

Put a knife to your throat if you are given to werewolfism. Until then, keep your feet on the ground, your head in the clouds and a beer mug to your lips, unless ye become drunken in which case, refer to the earlier proverbs.

Lycanthropy is derived from the Greek lykanthropos: wolf + human + the behavior of werewolfism. This refers to the fact that werewolfism is the ingestion of humans or anyone who is swallowed to the point of waste. In other words, when the moon is full, you might want to weigh your options before heading into the forest.

Socio-Economic Effects

With respect to werewolfism as it pertains to eating people, in lean times werewolfism was a sign of pride in the fact that if things ever got too bad, you could always eat your neighbor. In times of plenty, it was considered a byproduct of drinking and hunting too much. Either way it was always viewed as sinful and a real sneaky thing to do to your neighbors.

In a non-religious view of werewolfism, it can at least lead to health problems, including death by silver bullets, and heart disease from the fatty ripped-out throats of your overweight friends and family.

In many cultures, the love of werewolfism has caused a great number of citizens to grow obese, have excessive gas, and consume people they used to play cards with.

Theoretical Speculation

Beelzebub is the demon that the German bishop Peter Binsfield paired with the sin of werewolfism in 1589. This demon is said to be the specific tempter for this type of sin. Bishop Binsfield was later believed to be a werewolf himself. He was burned at the stake by several of his respected colleagues.

Considerations

Throughout history, werewolves plagued peasants. St. Gregory pointed out five ways to contract Lycanthropy—drinking the last swallow of beer from a stranger's mug, one-night stands, R-rated movies, condoms, and Facebook.

CHAPTER 5
THE CONTEMPORARY
WEREWOLF

Werewolves are lazy, greedy and gluttonous. Although still dangerous, the Contemporary Werewolf is much less ferocious than its ancient predecessors. Also, werewolves may still kill you.

In the old days, werewolves pretty much did two things—ripping out throats and running from angry mobs. But because of advances in our food distribution systems, grocery stores, restaurants etc, the modern werewolf tends to rip out fewer throats and do a lot more grocery shopping.

Werewolves eat an incredible amount of meat. Anyone you know who participates in excessive bulk grocery shopping is probably a werewolf. Below are formulas designed to assist you in determining whether or not a grocery shopper is a werewolf:

-100 lbs of bacon + Keg of DLB = werewolf

-Side of beef + 30lbs of Chicken legs = werewolf

-Dog food + DLB + Pork Rinds = werewolf

-Several of your loved ones chopped up in a freezer =werewolf.

Although bloodthirsty and condemned to Hell, today's modern werewolf enjoys many of the same lifestyle choices that us regular folks enjoy, including recreational activities like trail riding, water sports, and karaoke. Hiking and biking provide werewolves with the perfect disguise—a harmless human engaged in a peaceful activity. This is an effective technique by which werewolves hunt.

Snowmobiles and Werewolves

During snowmobile season, many of the trail riders you see throughout the U.P. are in fact werewolves. The full body suit and helmet offer a perfect disguise for any werewolf who has morphed.

Werewolves hit the trail pretty hard during the winter. If you know someone who spends an inordinate amount of time on his snowmobile for the winter months, there is great likelihood this person is a werewolf.

If this person is overweight, drinks DLB in excess and farts unusually loud and astringent farts, the odds of Lycanthropy are elevated. Do not confront this person. Follow this werewolf for the purpose of viewing and recording his behavior. We'll cover some of the best ways to do this in the *Tactics* section of this field guide.

Regarded as one of the nation's top snowmobiling states, Michigan has about 6,200 miles of groomed snowmobile trails, offering terrain of forest and field to both humans *and* werewolves. There are over 390,000 registered snowmobilers in Michigan. Of those, over fifty percent are werewolves.

In the past, these 195,000 werewolves were primarily responsible for regulating the population as the average adult werewolf can consume up to ninety other snowmobilers in a single winter.

Today, most werewolves are contemporary and choose to purchase their food at the grocery store, leaving the bulk of the throat ripping to one or two full-time werewolves. According to the Michigan Bureau of Werewolf Statistics, about 90% of all snowmobile throats that get ripped are the work of one or two werewolves.

Workwolves

An overworked werewolf can be much more dangerous than a werewolf on vacation or vice-versa. Friday nights are wild nights where unemployed werewolves clash with overworked werewolves. Werewolves love to go out on Friday night and blow off steam where they can engage in consuming DLB, overeating, or good old-fashioned fun. Throat ripping is considered good old-fashioned fun.

It should be noted that werewolves are not Hellhounds. Hellhounds are hounds born in hell. Werewolves are people born on earth but who are damned to hell. Both are very hell-like.

Werewolves can be dangerous any time of day but the contemporary werewolf has a high level of professionalism and may wait until after dark to have some good old-fashioned fun. Regardless of education level, any werewolf will be glad to eat you. Contemporary werewolves, although pacified by advances in food technology, still tend to be a lot less considerate than werewolves in the old days.

In the early eighteen hundreds it was common practice for werewolves to knock on a person's door. When the homeowner opened the door the werewolf would say, "Pardon thou, but I shall be needing to rip out thine throat."

The patron would either reply, "Leavest mine home beast, get thee thither," or "Run everybody!"

Both responses provoked attack but at least ample warning was provided.

In the twenty-first century, advanced warning is not the case as werewolves have become far too accustomed to a lack of social etiquette, like whipping the finger in traffic, killing you in the woods, or smart phones in restaurants.

CHAPTER 6
WEREWOLF
CHARACTERISTICS

No matter where you are in the U.P., there are werewolves in your area. Before you attempt any werewolfing whatsoever, you must first learn to identify possible werewolves. Most days of the month werewolves look just like ordinary people. But with a little experience, you can learn to profile a possible werewolf based on a person's characteristics. This includes both the physical and behavioral traits that seasoned werewolfers have learned to identify.

Physical Characteristics

Physical traits include the way a werewolf looks, sounds or smells. Before we discuss the physical traits of Upper Peninsula werewolves you must first learn to distinguish between the two types of changers:

Slow Changers—Change a little bit everyday until the moon is full and the cycle is complete.

Fast Changers—Look normal until the moon is full, then change all at once.

Behavioral Characteristics

Behavioral characteristics include how a werewolf acts. This can include, shopping, walking, eating out of garbage cans, snoring or any other type of obnoxious behavior.

Slow Changers—One of the keys to identifying slow changers is to examine people carefully. That means photos and observation from a distance. If you stare at someone very close to their face, they will become annoyed. They may punch you in the nose. Discreet werewolfers have an excellent sense of smell.

Fast Changers—When the moon is full, you better run like hell!

Eating You

Most werewolves who eat you prefer the method of throat ripping. Throat ripping is the manual ripping apart of the soft, blood engorged membrane on your neck with giant razor sharp fangs and claws.

This tender area is just below your chin. Put your hand on your throat right now and gently feel the blood engorged tissue. Delicious isn't it? Most werewolves agree. In fact, three out of four werewolves prefer the soft blood engorged membrane of your throat to sugarless gum.

Another popular method of eating you is dismemberment. Dismemberment is where the werewolf removes your arms, legs and head in a fury of claw, teeth and bone, driven to carnivorous bloodlust by the deepest, darkest parts of hell, and one heck of an attitude problem. The benefit of dismemberment is that the victim passes out, allowing the werewolf to kill other members of his party and then return later for a dismembered nighttime snack.

Many rogue species of werewolf will eat anything they can catch and choose to live in habitats where there is plenty of prey. Both northern and southern werewolves capture their prey on the run, killing and tearing them into smaller chunks with large and powerful mouthparts and claws. Once this process has begun it can be very difficult to stop.

While in human form, these Lycanthropes pose as people from your every day life, like the people you meet in nightclubs. During wolf-phase, they attack a broad range of people and other vertebrates.

If a werewolf attacks too many vertebrates in one specific area he may be killed by an angry mob. Get together with other people in your neighborhood and plan ahead for angry mob night. Decide who the organizers are going to be. Advance planning can be the difference between a memorable mob experience or a night of unforeseen tragedy, like blood and horror.

Some werewolves hunt in large cities among the homeless. If you are homeless, get together with other homeless people in your alley and organize your own angry mob. Angry mobs are a cheap efficient way to avenge the death of one of your peers. If your group cannot afford torches, you can make your own out of duct tape.

Urban werewolves are quite particular about what they eat and have specialized behaviors for locating their prey. Homeless people fit this category.

Aquatic werewolves must capture new supplies of fresh air to remain under water for hunting. Water werewolves do this by breaking through the surface headfirst.

Using their big werewolf ears to break through the water surface, they draw a layer of air over their body and store it in their lungs. Diving werewolves break through the surface with the tip of their werewolf nose to trap an air bubble. When the oxygen supply of the bubble is nearly exhausted, the werewolf must return to the surface for more air. Swimming in werewolf waters may be hazardous.

Werewolf Powers

Werewolves defend themselves from other predators using supernatural powers. For example, many large werewolves avoid being killed by shape-shifting or becoming too large or frightening in appearance.

Sharp claws and big, powerful jaws also protect them from things such as werewolf hunters, angry mobs, zombies, killer robots, ghosts, and of course, witches, although the existence of some of these creatures have not been proven.

Werewolves with shiny, metallic colors and bold patterns make some look less werewolf-like and hence are overlooked by angry mobs. Many werewolves are plain in color or have blotchy patches of browns, blacks, and grays that make them almost invisible when hiding in the bushes. Some werewolves are protected because they look or behave as your neighbor or the cable guy.

The chemical weapons of werewolves are produced by special glands or taken directly from their food. These foul-smelling and bad-tasting chemicals are released as gas, or exhaled breath. Bombardier werewolves spray a burning, stinging fluid out of their snowmobiles with surprising accuracy. They may also have silly names like Tuffie, Jabber, Hoyt or Big'n.

Basic Communication

Werewolves communicate using physical, visual, or chemical means, usually to find a mate. The best-known form of visual communication among werewolves is bioluminescence (BI-oh-LU-mih-NEH-sens), or light produced by their eyes. Each species has it own eye-flashing pattern. The number and speed of flashes help males and females of the same species recognize one another.

Males typically flash at night, flashing their eyes until they see a female respond with her own signal like, "How 'bout buying me a drink, Sailor," or "Is that a silver bullet in your pocket?"

Upon locating a female, the werewolf is relentless until the female either gives up or throws a drink in his face, or is cannibalized.

Characteristics and Physical Features for Werewolf Identification

Large werewolves are common in the U.P. They are noted for their red faces, long beards, domestic light beer, and slurring of words. These werewolves can be heard howling around the full moon or laughing unusually loud in local taverns. Werewolves are also scavengers and will eat decaying meat, fish, garbage, fecal matter, dead animals and any type of sausage you can think of. These materials are key if one is to successfully spot a werewolf. Werewolfing trips can take as little as an hour or as long as a football game.

Physical Characteristics

The following list of physical characteristics can be helpful in identifying your average werewolf:

Length: 4-7 ft. Weight: 130-440 lb.
Color:
White/Brown/Numerous/Bloody
Distinguishing Characteristics: Your severed arm inside its mouth.
Breeding: After wounding, or date night.
Habitat: Often behind you.
Range: The Arctic, Russia, Alaska, Canada, Greenland, Scandinavia, Germany, Florida and The Upper Midwest
Diet: People and other bulk meats.

Does the werewolf deserve its name?

Werewolves don't deserve squat! The name *werewolf* means hairy glutton. Werewolves satisfy their gluttony in many ways, like killing a person or buying thirty pounds of chicken legs. Werewolves may spray dead people with musk and bury them for later. Other werewolves order take-out.

Is the werewolf fast?

The werewolf has two speeds: fast and stop. If the werewolf is not sprinting, it is at a complete stop. Therefore, to catch prey the werewolf must ambush, pounce, or find a slower animal, like the lady up at the Salvation Army.

Why do werewolves run snowmobiles at their top speed? Going as fast as possible helps the werewolf stay on top of the snow in the winter. This must be done or it can't cover the distance it has to travel for finding DLB and other snowmobilers to eat. Also, going fast kicks ass.

What does the werewolf do if he is slower than his prey?

To attack prey, the werewolf will climb to the top of a rock or a tall stump, then, when a person or some other medium-to-large animal comes along, the werewolf will jump squarely on the throat of its victim. Many times the werewolf will disguise himself as someone you know.

Does the werewolf have any handicaps?

Werewolves pound the beers. This requires that they hunt in an ambush type manner. Pork rinds and bacon allow the werewolf to survive between hunts.

How big is a werewolf's territory?

The werewolf's territory can be extensive, sometimes reaching 200 square miles, but mostly it just goes to work and comes home. Sometimes a werewolf will leave his scent on hills and on rocks to say to other werewolves "Back off, this is my spot," or "Hey Mamma, let's party."

How do arctic people benefit from the werewolf?

The Alaska natives don't let any part of the werewolf go to waste. They prize the soft warm fur to keep them warm in subzero temperatures. This fur is used in making ruff for parkas. Werewolf fur has a durability rating of 1000, which means it's hairs are supernatural and do not break off, so it lasts for years. The problem is that as soon as the moon isn't full, it turns back into a person's skin hence the name "Meeknicki" or *Mooncoat* or *coat that only works once a month.*

Today, a variety of werewolf products and information is available that may permit us to enjoy these fascinating cannibalistic creatures from the inside out.

CHAPTER 7
WEREWOLF HEALTH FACTS

In today's modern industrialized society, werewolves now suffer from many of the same problems as their human counterparts. Diabetes, heart disease, high blood pressure high cholesterol and supernatural carnage are all on the increase among werewolves.

Obesity

Because werewolves love to eat and hate exercise, obesity rates among werewolves have skyrocketed. Remember, unlike vampires and zombies (no proof of existence) werewolves are not the risen undead, they are very much alive. Lycanthropy is a disease and people should be empathetic towards Lycanthropes, unless they are being attacked, in which case running, not empathy, is recommended.

Sleep Disorders

Sleep disorders are common among werewolves during the fuller moon cycles. Also, during these cycles werewolves may be killing you.

Oral Health

Werewolves hate dentists. If you know someone who hasn't been to the dentist in a wolf's age, they might be a werewolf. Conversely, some werewolves *are* dentists. If your dentist is never around during the full moon, it may be time to get a second opinion. If you experience a dental emergency during the full moon it is recommended that you ask your dentist for a local anesthetic instead of gas.

Due to their fear and hatred of dentists, chronic halitosis is at epidemic proportions among werewolves. If someone's breath at work smells like coffee and cigarettes, your boss may be a werewolf.

Athlete's Foot

Athlete's foot is also at epidemic proportions among werewolves. Because werewolf feet don't fit in their shoes after metamorphosis, they tend to walk around in bare feet. If someone you know has yellow brittle toenails and red itchy toes and walks around in bare feet a lot, he may be a werewolf. Also, anyone with blood and gore smeared all over their face could be a werewolf.

Personal Hygiene

Werewolves have tremendous body odor. If you are in the grocery store or retail center or perhaps some other public place and you smell someone with really bad BO, there's a good chance of werewolfism. The funny thing is that werewolves can't smell themselves. They don't even know that they smell bad. Also, many werewolves may know they smell bad, but still don't care.

Farting

Werewolf farts are loud and astringent. If you smell a profoundly loud, astringent fart in the Upper Peninsula, it is probably from a werewolf. Even if it is from someone you believe to be a family member or loved one.

In the U.P. werewolves have managed to infiltrate every level of society. Make sure you know whom that farter in the living room recliner really is. Ask yourself these questions:

Is this a recent phenomenon?
How did I end up here?

In order to identify a werewolf fart we must first define the terms loud and astringent.

Loud

By *loud* we mean not quiet and more than just above silent. I mean loud, like a jackhammer or a machine gun, where the noise is so loud and repetitive it's like it will never stop rattling inside your ears, nose and throat. Perhaps your ears ring afterward or several of the glasses in your kitchen cabinets shatter.

If the forceful vapor split the person's pants, that would also constitute a loud fart, and so would any other question the fart may have raised in your mind, for example:

Am I safe being in close proximity to that much methane?

Will my hearing be permanently affected by this?

Could something that sounds like a Harley Davidson really come out of a living creature?

All of these questions would be accurate symptoms of *loud* and hence werewolfism.

Astringent

If the smell of the fart wilts flowers or creates static on your television set or burns your eyes like an onion, we would define it as astringent. If the fart is so thick you need fog lights, that would also fit the definition.

If you suffer any of the following symptoms as a result of the powerful smell—hair loss, backaches, Crone's disease, Fibromyalgia, Colitis, low-grade fever or vomiting—a Lycanthropic source is possible.

Identifying Werewolf Farts

Difficulty identifying werewolf farts can occur when a smelly person lives in your house, say a father or grandfather or a big fat uncle. While not always Lycanthropes, these men have been known to put out a considerable number of astringent farts. To be sure, you must confront this person during one of these instances. Say something direct and inquisitive, for example:

Grandfather, are you a werewolf or do you need a dietician?

Father, are you a werewolf or are you spraying for bugs?

Uncle, are you a werewolf or should I fetch some adult undergarments?

Conscientious werewolfers can gain valuable insight right in their own homes. In addition to gas, being torn to pieces by one of your family members beneath the full moon may be an indication of werewolfism.

CHAPTER 8
WEREWOLFING DO'S AND DON'TS

Michigan's Upper Peninsula is all about the great outdoors, the fresh air, the Great Lakes, and the werewolves. With its wide-open spaces, unique attractions, and unlimited supernatural opportunities, it is the ideal werewolf watching territory, unmatched in disappearances anywhere in the Midwest!

Festivals and events are sure to add even more enjoyment throughout the entire year, like Werewolf Octoberfest. This event is usually held during the first full moon in

September proving that werewolves don't own calendars.

Identifying werewolves can be challenging. Werewolves are supernatural creatures and you need a quick eye to spot as many details as possible. There are many obstacles. The light may be dim, you could have the sun in your eyes, or the werewolf may be trying to eat your internal organs. You'll want to know what to look for, what matters most, and how to report your own death.

When you spot a werewolf, don't immediately try to flip through the pages of a field guide to identify it. Keep your eye fixed on the werewolf and study it. Absorb the details of its markings, movements, habits, and size. You may want to jot down notes like, "Is that thing going to kill me?" or "I bet that thing could eat a person and wash it down with forty bratwursts."

Don't focus too much on your jottings. Try to maximize the time you have with the werewolf in view. This is your time to study the beast and you don't know how long it will be before it leaves, or spots you. Listening for a werewolf's howl is simple, but it's also easy to forget to do. If you don't make a conscious effort to listen, you won't remember the werewolf's howl and you'll miss out on one of the best werewolf identification tools there is.

The good news is that you can listen to a werewolf while you watch it. Look for the profile of the Lycanthrope or listen for the screaming horror of a flesh-ripped victim just to ensure you're associating the correct noise with the correct creature.

A general picture of the werewolf, and its approximate size and shape will often give you many clues when placing it into the correct family of supernatural shape-shifters. Therefore, begin with an assessment of the werewolf's overall appearance. What is the approximate size of the werewolf?

It's easiest to estimate size in relation to people. For instance, is the werewolf you're observing about the size of a professional football player or the size of a professional jockey? A fat janitor or a slinky palm-reader? A square accountant or your slobby Uncle Steve?

Think in terms of silhouettes and try to get an idea of the general body shape. Does it seem calm, or is it salivating and gaining on you? After determining size and shape, you're ready to start noticing details. Start at the head. Does it have evil red eyes or horns? Is the facial fur matted with the blood and flesh of your friend?

Also, note the color and shape of the werewolf's mouth. How long is it in relation to the werewolf's head? Is it straight or curved, conical or flattened? Are their chewed entrails? Is the mouth docile or is it wide open and coming towards you at horrific speed?

Next, look for details on the werewolf's tail. Keep an eye out for its razor-sharp claws. What color are its back and belly? How long is its tail in relation to the werewolf's body length? How does it hold its tail? Does it have a bushy tail or is it shorthaired? Are the claws tearing into your throat or are they at a safe distance? Can you see your own headless body lying on the ground?

Now study the werewolf's legs. Does the werewolf have long legs or short legs? What color are its legs? Are the legs propelling the werewolf towards you in a manner that indicates it may kill you? Some werewolves even have toes that are arranged quite different than others and if you're fortunate enough to have a close-up view, you may briefly notice one of these differences before perishing.

Observe the way the werewolf walks, how it holds its tail, or how it jumps from the bushes toward your throat. Does it swoop down upon your head or does it glide gently and steadily toward you?

Try to determine who else the werewolf is eating or has eaten. Does it cling to a tree and then pummel your head? Does it forage across your lawn, tilting its head before attack? Does it hide nearby in a pond? Did the amount of blood leaving your body surprise you?

Make note of the habitat in which you have observed the werewolf. You can do this even after the werewolf has eaten parts of you. Did you spot the werewolf in a wetland or woodland? Are you in an urban setting or a farm field? Each species of werewolf has a typical region they inhabit. Take note of the region you're in when you observe a werewolf. Also, werewolves migrate throughout the seasons, so make note of the time of year or specific date you observe the werewolf.

Jot down your observations for later reference when you get out of the hospital. From markings to behavior, write down anything you noticed. All of these things can help when you sit down with a field guide to confirm the werewolf's species. Also, write down any stories that may be funny.

CHAPTER 9
TACTICS FOR BETTER
WEREWOLFING

Now that you have a list of equipment and some general background information about werewolves, let's try and spot a few.

Ambushing Werewolves

Waylaying Lycanthropes may be an offbeat tactic, but the rush is unbeatable. Stalking werewolves, although a hardy and invigorating pursuit, is not every Wolfologist's cup of tea. For instance, physical limitations might prevent a fellow from sprinting uphill to prevent throat ripping, or another werewolfer might prefer to take a stand, administering his own last rights.

What makes many watchers' blood boil is the sudden appearance of a distant werewolf and its subsequent attack. Many have attempted to stalk werewolves because nothing gets the heart pounding like a good bum-rush.

I cannot overemphasize the importance of being quiet. One small mistake and your day can turn upside down. Because of this, we will first attempt some novice-level werewolfing.

Novice-level werewolfing involves the use of some type of structure that provides safety from the werewolf. This allows you to jot down details without massive blood loss. Below is a list of structures and their dependability.

Cabins

Although shoddy in appearance, for some reason creepy, woodland cabins seem to offer supernatural protection from any werewolf that doesn't actually live there. Werewolves tend to prefer the forest during metamorphosis and are reluctant to enter cabins. At most, they may stick an arm through a boarded up window or try to peel away parts of the roof. Then they give up and leave.

If you see a werewolf entering someone else's cabin he may be ill. To report sick werewolves visit:

www.wheresmylefthand.com.

Outhouses

Outhouses attract werewolves and should not be used. Nothing tickles a werewolf's fancy like tearing the crap out of someone.

Tents

Tents are worse than outhouses—see outhouses.

Maintenance Sheds

Because they're often distracted by weed whackers, mowers, snow blowers and other types of loud equipment, maintenance men have become a favorite food of werewolves and should be avoided. Empty maintenance sheds, however, offer protection for any werewolfer on the run.

If you are hiding in an empty maintenance shed and a maintenance man returns, make some type of excuse that encourages him to leave, such as: "Hey, those kids on the other side of the park are throwing beer bottles on your grass."

Or,

"Someone dropped their wallet over by the barbecue pit."

Or,

"One of your guys left the hedge-trimmers in the woods."

Anything that will put some yards between you and that maintenance man will work in your favor. This is called baiting. We will we be discussing baiting later. Also, maintenance men may often be werewolves.

Abandoned farms

Abandoned farms are a common sight in the Upper Peninsula and can be used for hiding if they are not haunted. However, haunted abandoned farms may house werewolves. If you are unsure whether an abandoned farm is haunted, consult a psychic or ask around the neighborhood before using it as a werewolfing sanctuary.

It should be noted that certain restrictions apply when werewolfing on private property.

Cars

Cars offer some protection from werewolves and are great for making out. Also, werewolves eat people while they are making out in cars.

To properly use a car for werewolfing, keep the engine running and have an extra set of keys in the glove compartment.

Straw/Stick Houses

Straw and Stick houses offer no protection as werewolves have learned to huff and puff and blow these structures down.

Brick Houses

Brick houses offer excellent werewolf protection but werewolves are never around them. See werewolf hot spots.

Following Suspected Werewolves

Werewolves must be followed during non-metamorphosed hours. People infected with Lycanthropy change from humans into ferocious beasts when the full moon glows, but this doesn't always occur overnight.

Some werewolves change a little bit each day for the course of the month until the moon becomes full, and only then does the change become complete. We must differentiate these two groups.

Slow Changers.

The easiest Lycanthropes to watch are Slow Changers. Because of a mutated werewolf Chromosome, these werewolves are affected by the daily moon changes. For example, an infected person may grow a much thicker mustache and beard as the month wears on, or appear to not have had a hair cut in a long time when actually it's only a couple of days' growth.

After another week goes by, you may hear this person say something like, "I'll be back. I have to grow a tail."

Fast Changers.

Fast changers are tough to watch because they exhibit very few physical warning signs. The moon becomes completely full and whammo, they turn into the beast we love to be killed by. Werewolfers must be sensitive when following any suspected werewolf.

If all you have to go on are werewolf-type habits and no real physical proof, refrain from killing them. If they attempt to kill you, do not refrain from killing them.

Werewolfing Chart

On the following page is a sample chart for detecting suspected werewolves. Run off copies of this chart or make up your own. Keep track of all vital information on the suspected Lycanthrope.

NAME	TIME OF DAY	PLACE
John Doe-wolf	10:00 am	Grocery Store
CHARACTERISTICS EXHIBITED		

1. Subject purchased forty pounds of chicken leg-quarters, sixty pounds of hamburger meat, canned anchovies in mustard sauce, ten bags of potato chips and three cases of Domestic Light Beer.

2. Subject wore a cut-off flannel button-down shirt.

3. Subject had extremely hairy arms and pits.

4. Subject was not wearing deodorant.

5. Subject's feet, although covered with shoes, were probably disgusting.

6. Subject looked ridiculous and dirty.

7. Subject grumbled unintelligible things when the clerk presented him with his total.

8. Subject had to return several bags of potato chips because he was short on cash.

9. Subject's wallet was possibly made out of human skin.

10. Subject is either a werewolf or Larry The Cable Guy.

FOLLOW?	Yes

Figure 1. Werewolfing Chart

Notice how the information is listed in numerical order. Try to be detail-oriented. Not only is it important to list the facts, but also to put the facts into some kind of perspective, such as a *Larry The Cable Guy* reference

Other Methods

After years of werewolfing, you may have come up with your own way to keep track of possible werewolves. Figure 2. (next page) is the type of chart kept by Arthur T. Picket, one of the fastest running werewolfers known throughout the world.

Before his disappearance in 2012, Picket was said to have out-run nineteen of the twenty werewolves he spotted. He credited his great success, we think, to the fact that he numbered suspected werewolves and cross-referenced them, thus allowing him to maximize his werewolfing opportunities.

Picket kept a separate list of characteristics and then numbered the werewolves in order of highest likelihood to lowest. Working backwards, Picket eliminated each suspect, narrowing it down to one actual werewolf.

#	Date	Location Followed	Result
1	7/3/012	National Forest	Just a redneck
2	7/4/012	BP Station	Just a hick
3	7/10/012	My Property	Not sure, will follow
4	7/11/012	Far Away from cabin	Possible Were-wolf
5	7/11/012	Behind Cabin	. . . help!
6	7/11/012	. . . ahhhh!	

Figure 2. The Picket Chart

Experts believe Picket disappeared somewhere between 7/11/12 and 7/12/12, but no one can be certain. The point is that he kept good records.

More Tactics For Following Werewolves

It is important that the suspected werewolf does not see you following him. The tactics listed below have been compiled from some of the World's leading werewolfers.

The Car Slouch

Sitting in your car, watching werewolves in secret is the number one way to follow a suspected Lycanthrope. If anyone cruises past you just slide down in your seat until your head is below window level. If the type of car you drive prohibits full slouching, dress in a tourist disguise and pretend you're reading a map.

Be sure you have some type of prop such as a map. A prop enables you to sell the illusion that you're doing something. If you half-slouch, someone may ask you what you're doing. If you have no prop, you may say something stupid like, "I was just, um, ... thinking about this ... napkin," or "Oh, I misplaced my ... parrot."

To ensure better observation through slouching, watch old episodes of the seventies TV show *The Rockford Files*.

Dumpster Diving

The good old garbage industry is always there when you need them. You may never be able to find a cop when you need one, but that big old smelly garbage truck will for sure be there on Tuesday, barring any legal holidays of course.

If there is a good dumpster at the gas station or retail center near you, it can be a great place to conceal yourself and *pick up on* suspected werewolves. If you don't mind garbage, this may be a solid option. Also, werewolves eat out of dumpsters.

The Bushes

People have been hiding in the bushes since caveman days. Unfortunately, werewolves have been eating people in the bushes since the caveman days.

Urban/Rural Camouflage

Camouflage or "Cammo" allows a person to blend in to their surroundings. The principle of cammo is that objects are identified by their outlines. If you break up your own outline, you are much more difficult to identify. For example, if you wish to hide in front of the grocery store, you may want to dress like a bag of groceries or a shopping cart. Also, do not disguise yourself as a parking space or you may be injured.

In the forest, proper woodland cammo is recommended. These cammos are available at any werewolf equipment retailer near you.

Tree Stands

In the past, werewolfers used the same type of tree stands that hunters use, as werewolves cannot climb trees. Unfortunately, werewolves *can* rip trees out of the ground. This was proven true in early

2003 by Dr. Peter Klanjiic of Menominee, MI, last seen in March of that year.

Ground Blinds

Although ground blinds offer great camouflage for the experienced werewolfer, they offer very little protection for the novice werewolfer. See tents and outhouses.

Armored Vehicles

The best way to view a werewolf on the move is from inside an armored vehicle. Armored vehicles offer great protection against werewolves and other monsters as well as roadside bombs, machine gun fire, rocket propelled grenades and most domestic populations engaged in civil unrest.

Baiting Werewolves

Baiting werewolves is a great way to instantly make a positive I.D. on a werewolf. Trick someone into a dangerous situation and then record what happens. Although legal in The Upper Peninsula of Michigan, werewolf-baiting laws vary from state to state.

Be sure to consult your State Mythological Monster Commission for details on what the law is in your county. For more information go to:

wheresmylefthand.com.

The Bait and Switch

This tactic involves the use of a dummy or decoy body. Simply buy a lifelike dummy at any dummy outlet store. Paint the throat of the dummy like it's bloody or perhaps place a couple of packages of chicken thighs around it. Set it out in the open and hide in your armored car with your telephoto lens. Werewolves will almost always go for a dummy that smells like chicken thighs. Also, if chicken thighs sit out in the sun do not eat them.

Trap door

A trap door is a great way to confuse any werewolf. Trap doors allow a werewolfer to hide underground safely while baiting or observing. You can build your own trap door by digging a six-foot diameter hole and covering it with a hinged, wooden spring loaded door. If you cannot afford a trap door, make your own out of duct tape.

Sorcery

One of the best tactics in werewolf watching is the use of sorcery. Sorcery has been around since the dawn of time and is one of the primary control techniques for viewing werewolves. Sorcery allows you to cast a spell on a werewolf, making that particular lycanthrope your minion.

This can be very effective as everyone *loves* a minion and minions are always great at parties.

For example:

"Hey minion, go get some more beer, eh?"

"Yes Master."

Below is a sample from Einrid Slaarljjk, one of the top sorcerer/werewolfers in his time. Einrid wrote:

"Aye I have him now, locked in the embrace of mine magic spell. He stands before me looking as if he wishes to eat me, yet I control him with three simple words .... ickny, racknite ... uh ... what was ye other word? ... oh crap. I'm losing it ... ahhhh . . ."

If you are not familiar with sorcery, consult these books:

Practicing Sorcery in Michigan's Upper Peninsula, by Dale R. Hoffman.

Reading Palms in the U.P., by Dale R. Hoffman.

Michigan Crystal Ball Forecasting, by Dale R. Hoffman.

Incantations, Augury, and Conjuring in Michigan's Upper Peninsula, by Dale R. Hoffman.

CHAPTER 10
DEALING WITH NUISANCE WEREWOLVES

If you live in a werewolf-populated area, you know how much werewolves love to root around in your garbage. Nothing is more annoying than waking up in the morning only to find that werewolves have been in your trash again.

Because werewolves are half-human, they are not susceptible to standard bear and raccoon-proofing. However, there are a number of products on the market today to deter nuisance werewolves. Remember, werewolves can be fooled, thus preventing interference with home and garden. If you're tired of cleaning up after these bad news werewolves, take steps to keep them away from your garbage cans.

For example, use werewolf-proof garbage containers. These have Vaseline-covered lids, making it difficult for the werewolves to get inside them. Werewolves cannot crush or rip the reinforced sides, tops and bottoms. Also, store your garbage cans in your garage or shed. Separate food waste from non-food garbage and keep discarded corpses in a garage or shed until garbage pick-up day.

Reduce odors that can attract werewolves to your cans. Clean garbage cans regularly using disinfectants, bleach, silver bullets, or anything that isn't blood-based. Spray the inside of your cans with ammonia between cleanings to help discourage future werewolves. Also, play some Jon Tesh over a loudspeaker.

Inspecting For Lycanthropes

People become werewolves when bitten, but that is not how werewolves breed. Lycanthropes breed with other werewolves in damp organic material such as garbage piles, dead animals and sleazy motel rooms. If large numbers of these lycanthropes are found in a single area, it may be a sign of an infestation. Look for hundreds of spent beer-cans, cigarette butts or pieces of dead people. Outdoors, inspect the area for even more dead bodies.

Sanitation measures not only include cleaning garbage containers and dumpsters, but also moving such containers as far as possible from buildings and making sure that dead friends and relatives are buried to the proper depth. Check dumpsters for properly fitting anti-werewolf lids. Keep areas around dumpsters clean and dry.

If a large amount of dead bodies begin to pile up, place these people in sealed garbage bags, then properly dispose of them outdoors, preferably in werewolf-proof containers. Breeding lycanthropes have also been found in compost piles and animal feces.

Exclusion of werewolves involves properly locked doors and windows and any spells you may cast. Check for areas where supernatural creatures have easy access to the building. Seal all cracks around doors and walls where even large lycanthropes can squeeze through.

In cases where there are battles between good and evil, baiting should be used to deter lycanthropes. Sacrificial human bait should be re-applied after every blood feast or rainfall. Are there homeless people going through your offerings at night? If so, they may transform. Sacrifice them just in case. Remember to make human sacrifices around windows and doors where lycanthropes linger.

Sprays can be helpful tools in eliminating nuisance werewolves, but the elimination of their breeding sources is the only guaranteed way to eliminate them. Make certain all possible human sacrifice measures have been implemented before relying on chemical sprays to eliminate lycanthropes.

WEREWOLFING PRODUCTS

1. Werewolf-Proof Garbage Bin, $39.95, available at Wolfco.

Heavy-duty aluminum frame and molded hard plastic panels with hidden combination locks under front panel. Werewolves' fat furry fingers can't detect the combination locks.

Guaranteed to drive any nuisance werewolf crazy, as in, "How the crap do I get this thing open?"

Holds up to six, thirty-gallon trashcans, available in forest green or woodland brown.

Custom finishes also available for an additional $9.95 and include two motifs:

a. *Rising Sun motif*

Proven to scare post-metamorphosis werewolves and possibly vampires, although the existence of vampires has not been proven.

b. *TV Show, The View motif*

Mural features the entire old cast, including Whoopie and Rosie O'Donnell. Pull the string and the cast blabs for up to forty-eight hours. Even the most seasoned werewolf can't listen to that garbage and would rather go find some *other* garbage.

2. **Werewolf Decoys, $13.95, available at The Modern Werewolf.**

Plastic life-size look-alike werewolves lure unsuspecting werewolves away from garbage area.

Multiple styles are available and include:

a. *Snow-bunny Werewolf Decoy*

Hit that werewolf where it hurts, right in the family jewels. Werewolves spend night and day attempting to *pick up* the decoy. By the time he realizes she's plastic, it's already trash day.

b. *Hollow Snowmobile Decoy*

Werewolf thinks he's found a *fixer upper* and spends night and day tinkering. Eventually, the werewolf tires of buying replacement parts and abandons the area for the season.

c. *Agent With Book Deal Decoy*

Motion activated fake book-deal offer, works on werewolf's over-inflated ego. Werewolf spends the week talking about himself instead of going through your trash. 9 x 12 mirror included.

SPRAYS AND REPELLENTS

1. **Repellent Liquids**: Pour these around your garbage cans or trash area.

a. *Vegetarian Pee*

Nothing disgusts a werewolf more than the urine of vegetarians. Comes in carrot or asparagus. **$8.95 at Were-Mart.**

b. *Hot DLB Smell*

Smells like the day after the big party. Werewolves can't stand a hot dead soldier of a beer, especially one that's infused with the smell of a soggy old cigarette butt floater. **$12.95 at Home Werewolf.**

2. **Repellent Sprays:** Concentrated formulas for spraying around your garbage area.

a. *R.S. Sweat*™

Bottled spray contains the actual sweat from Richard Simmons during a taping of one of his workout videos in the eighties. That's thirty-year-old sweat! Includes a recording that frightens werewolves away with scratchy high-pitched "Let's go girls!" quips. **$9.95 at K-Wolf.**

WEREWOLVES AND LIVESTOCK

Farmers and werewolves have a long relationship with each other. Throughout the centuries farmers have blamed werewolves for the death of livestock and/or family members. Because of this mistrust farmers often kill or become werewolves.

We now know that many of the sheep and cattle slayings that farmers blamed on werewolves are alien spaceships performing experiments (see: *Welcoming Extraterrestrials To Your U.P. Farm,* by Dale R. Hoffman).

Although based in logic, this theory is not accepted by many cattle ranchers regardless of how many people say to them, "Hey I think aliens from a spaceship slaughtered your cow," or, "Look Dude, I saw a spaceship flying around your field last night!" or, "Haven't you ever seen *Independence Day?* Man, those things are ugly!"

Many farmers who *do* believe in Aliens have been subjected to ridicule and have chosen to kill werewolves because of an aversion to creatures damned to hell and/or because of the killing of one of their family members. Below is a list of commercial equipment available for protecting cattle and other livestock.

1. Werewolf Prod by Jigsen.

Zap that nuisance werewolf right on his backside and watch him run—or attack you! Uses one nine-volt battery (not included). Durable lightweight construction features super-strong cast aluminum shaft and reinforced steel electrodes. Extender pole enables farmer to hide inside a car or building and poke werewolf from up to twelve feet away.

2. **Fake Cow, by Farmfakes.**

Solid-state hollow cow enables farmer to hide comfortably inside while confusing werewolves with distracting calls such as, "Hey werewolf, look over there!" or "Ain't no moo-cow over here, werewolf!" or "Aaahhhh!"

Battery operated ears (two AA batteries not included) allow cow to appear realistic and unsuspecting. Use in conjunction with a werewolf prod and give 'em a jab. Nothing confuses a werewolf like a hollow cow with a prod sticking out, especially under cover of darkness. Also, werewolves can see in the dark and may attack the cow. **$99.95. Available at Farmfakes.com.**

3. Sheep-Full-O'-Tacks by Farmfakes.

"My what big lamb chops you have, Grandma." That's because it's not Grandma, it's Sheep-Full-O'-Tacks! Nothing ruins a werewolf's day like chomping down on the plumpest sheep in the herd and realizing it's full of sharp pointy objects.

Think one of your neighbors is a werewolf? Look for the guy with the poke-holes on his lips. If his lips leak when he eats soup, there's no denying it! **$59.95. Available at <u>Farmfakes.com</u>.**

4. Giant Bologna by Ingmar Mayer.

No self-respecting werewolf would eat livestock when there's a perfectly delicious oversized bologna hanging from a tree out back. Werewolves are attracted to the large skin casing of ground meat by-products and forget all about cattle or sheep.

Secret blue dye-pack inside explodes when eaten. "Hey Ned, how come your face is blue?"

Available at **WEREWOLVES-R-US** $4.99/lb.

WEREWOLF FENCING.

Although expensive, werewolf fencing has been proven to protect landowners and ranchers from nuisance werewolves. Two-hundred-fifty-foot-high fencing completely encircles any rancher's property to the limit of their legal air space. Werewolves simply get tired of climbing and turn around.

Works like a charm, but at six-hundred-dollars a square foot, be prepared to shell out some dough. Also, if a family member is a werewolf they may already be inside the fencing.

WEREWOLF LANDMINES.

Terrify werewolves with a Werewolf Landmine from Osakco™ Corp. Landmines adhere only to the furry foot of a werewolf and are not activated by the hooves of cattle or human shoes. Bury three to four of these beauties amidst the herd and kick back with a beer. And don't worry because there isn't any shrapnel in these land mines, just cologne and deodorant, two things that drive werewolves nuts! **Available at Osakco.com $29.99/pair.**

PIT OF DESPAIR.

There's nothing like catching a werewolf red-handed. Giant, hundred-foot hole traps werewolves in the ground until they re-morph in the morning. Hole-kit includes shovel, water bottle and towel for wiping sweat. Available at Wolfgreen's.

CHAPTER 11
EXTREME WEREWOLFING

With the advent of extreme sports, many in the younger generation have taken to extreme werewolfing. Extreme werewolfing is a high-octane version of werewolfing that involves a lot less hiding and a lot more direct contact with werewolves.

As the culture of throat ripping has evolved, so have the methods for record keeping. As with skate boarding, an entire new vocabulary of tricks has been developed. You may be killed performing these tricks so it is always best to work in pairs and have a voucher. Remember, when doing any extreme werewolfing use the buddy system.

Positive Tricks—performed when a werewolfer lives.

Looksy

This trick occurs any time you see a werewolf and survive. Good watch!

Cabin Grabbin'

This trick occurs any time you and your friends flee from a werewolf and survive by making it to some type of structure like a cabin. The werewolf pounds at the windows but for some reason he can't get in—award major points.

Sneak-A-Peak

Werewolfers observe a werewolf in his natural habitat for over ten minutes. Maybe the werewolf is one of your neighbors and you and your friend spy him through the window of his laboratory, shape-shifting or working with his evil minion. After observation, werewolfers sneak off and discuss the possibility of being attacked.

Watch-A-Thon

Occurs when someone in your house is a werewolf and you live to tell the tale. This is the person you eat and sleep with . . . and you're still alive? Amazing! 100 points.

The Defender

This occurs when a werewolfer successfully defends himself against attack by killing the werewolf. Award extra points for any of these styles of The Defender:

<u>The Silver</u>: Bullet through the heart. Works every time.
<u>The Crusher</u>: Squashed with anything heavy.
<u>The Chopper</u>: Decapitation.
<u>The Stickler</u>: Any impalement.
<u>Bon Voy'age</u>: Water death.

Minion Buster

Minion Buster occurs when you destroy a werewolves' minion in advance of encountering the werewolf. Killing an evil minion is also a great way to warm up for your next werewolf outing. 25 points.

Negative Tricks—performed when a werewolfer does not live.

180 Noggin Air

The werewolf watcher's head comes up in the air, spins one hundred-eighty-degrees, and briefly comes to rest back on the neck-stump before full-body collapse. It's not eyes in the back of your head—it's eyes in the front of your head in the back of your head.

360 Noggin Air

Same as 180 but all the way around—didn't I see that before? Remember, the head must briefly come to rest on the neck stump before collapse. As with all extreme sports moves, it doesn't count unless you land it.

920 Noggin Air

Performed only once by Tony "Wolf-man" Hawkins, last seen in 2010 performing the trick.

Noggin Number Air

This occurs when you witness your headless corpse hit the ground. You may only witness this briefly as your head has been knocked high into the air and this is usually accompanied by the high velocity spinning of said head. As your head spins, count the number of times you see your headless corpse lying on the ground. The number of times you count before your head hits the ground is your *Noggin Number*, as in "Whoa, Noggin—12! Awesome!"

Wheresy Air—Lefty and Righty

As in, "Where's my left hand?" or "Where's my right hand?" After dismemberment at the wrist, a werewolfer must yell at the top of his lungs, "Wheresy!" before the severed hand can hit the ground. If you cannot announce "Wheresy!" before the appendage hits the ground it does not count. Have your hand re-attached and try again later.

Wheresy—Bye-bye

Same as *Wheresy Air* but with an added trick—while your hand is falling to the ground, the hand waves goodbye. Spastic waves on the ground do not count.

Army Air

Same as Bye-bye but with the entire arm attached. Because it is so frequent, left and right do not matter.

Footsy Air—Lefty and Righty

A Wheresy with your foot but instead of yelling "Wheresy" you must yell "Footsy." Five points plus five points awarded for each toe that remains intact for a total of thirty.

Land Shark—Lefty and Righty

This move is performed when a werewolf bites one of your legs completely off as you flee. So close to surfing you'll swear that you're drenched in some type of liquid. As you lie on the ground remember that unlike a shark, the werewolf is not curious about what you are.

Thrasher—Lefty and Righty

Same as a Land Shark but your leg is thrown into the air in a murderous rage.

Thrasher/Howl

Same as Thrasher but as the leg is thrown into the air the beast releases the howl of a bloodthirsty creature damned to hell.

Rip Gurgle

As a werewolf attacks you, you may scream uncontrollably at high volume. If your throat is ripped during this high volume scream and the scream turns into a bubbly-sounding gurgle, award yourself ten points.

The Tribal

The Tribal is when a werewolf removes your scalp completely. Your brain may be exposed, leaving you to stand around scratching your head wondering why you can't scratch your head.

The Patsy

This occurs any time someone falls in love with a werewolf even though they know that person is a werewolf and is later killed by that werewolf. The Patsy will trump all other moves. Any points will be erased.

Buster Minion

The opposite of a Minion Buster and the oldest trick in the book. With the aid of his minion, the werewolf kills you via any of the previous means. Trumps all tricks. Remove all points.

Use these general guidelines and make up your own moves and games with your friends. As with all extreme sports, being good requires years of practice and hard work and the extra time that comes along with only being employed part-time.

CHAPTER 12
INTERVENTIONS

An intervention is a surprise meeting where concerned family and friends confront an individual werewolf out of love and respect. Werewolves are magnificent creatures and many of them suffer from the same types of problems us regular folks suffer from. If you suspect one of your friends is a werewolf, follow this twelve-step plan for intervention.

Twelve Step Intervention Plan For Lycanthropy

1. Identify the werewolf.

Confront the individual and accuse him of being a werewolf. If the individual kills and eats several of your loved ones at this meeting, you are ready for step two.

2. Reach out.

At the intervention you may be attacked. Reach out for anything within your grasp that you can use to help your situation—a gun, a baseball bat, phone, anything within arms reach.

If your arm is not attached, use your good arm to grab the dismembered arm and reach out with that. If your arm is not within reach of your good arm, reach out with your leg and kick the arm towards you, then reach out with your good arm and grab the dismembered arm.

Once you have reached out to your bad arm with your good arm, you should be able to reach for things up to one foot further than if your bad arm was still attached. Reach out to anything within that distance.

3. Engage.

If you would like to engage the individual werewolf with pleasant reassurances and a positive attitude, this method is encouraged. Also, you could engage them with a shotgun. If there is a vehicle in the driveway, engage the engine, then engage the transmission and flee.

Try to engage some of the other people and convince them to stay behind at the intervention. This will give you an opportunity to return later, after the creature's bloodlust has been quelled with several friends and family. Continue engaging in the program with all those who are still alive.

4. Acceptance

The downfall of all werewolves is thinking they can fight the power of the moon. Every month it's the same thing, the moon gets full, they go on a murderous rampage, they wake up naked at the zoo and then for some reason they think it's not going to happen again next month.

You must convince the werewolf that he is powerless to fight the moon. This will lead to an acceptance that the werewolf must change on his own.

Also, there are many methods of acceptance. One method is to reassure your friend that even though he's a creature damned to hell, there are many earthly options still open to him

Another method of acceptance is where you accept the fact that your friend is a werewolf and kill him in his sleep with a steel shovel. If you choose to kill your friend, be sure to complete the rest of the program anyway.

5. Create a non-twelve-step program

Some of the newest methods of treatment these days are non-twelve-step programs. These are un-numbered programs that allow more leeway and individual control of the supernatural process of healing.

To create a non-twelve-step program, create a twelve-step program full of methods and titles and governing principles. When your program is drawn up, delete the entire thing and do whatever you want. You are now one of the cutting edge leaders in American medicine today.

6. Draw A Pentagram

As I mentioned earlier, sorcery is a great way to control an infected lycanthrope. Magic spells are hard to find and often quite expensive so here is one of the best spells I have come across:

Draw a pentagram out of salt on the floor of your living room. Any salt will do, but I prefer coarse, kosher salt. I also prefer a bottle of tequila and a few lime wedges. You must place the werewolf inside the pentagram and then attach a few squirrel feathers to your ceiling fan. Turn the fan cycle on low. Now repeat this phrase:

Itchy, Scratchy, Popeye, Bluto, Tom and Jerry, Mr. Magoo. Scooby-dooby-dooby-do. Bugs and Daffy, Elmer too.

Also, if the werewolf is still killing you, the spell did not work. Try again later.

7. Memory Aid

You have to remind the werewolf that he is only human, except for that very small part of him that is damned and bloodthirsty. Remind the werewolf of all the good times you had before he became infected. Try to get the werewolf to think about his childhood or his love life.

At the end of the film *An American Werewolf in London*, nurse Alex Price attempts to reason with the werewolf David. She says,

"David please. I love you." And for a moment, the terrifying eyes of the creature soften, but then of course, he tries to kill her and is shot dead by London Police. Her effort failed because she skipped to step seven instead of including step seven in a broader, twelve-step plan for werewolf intervention.

8. Casual Friday

Casual Friday is a great way to break up the monotony of intervening in a supernatural infection. It's also a great way for those at the intervention to keep any blood and gore off their nice work clothes. Our statistics have shown that having your werewolf intervention on casual Friday is three to four times more likely to lead to a positive werewolf result.

Casual Friday creates an atmosphere of camaraderie and self-esteem, but some research indicates that full moon Fridays and Friday the thirteenths may be up to nine times more dangerous for intervening than regular Fridays. There is not enough data to know for sure.

9. Back Rub

Back rubs are a cheap and easy way to earn someone's trust. Ask your suspected werewolf if someone in your group can give a back rub. While you're rubbing, feel for mutating flesh and muscle beneath your hands. Bubbly skin can be a sign. See if there are any other signs, like bones cracking into animal shapes and long needlepoint hair popping out. Also, if any one has any Steely Dan, this is the time to play it.

10. Smoke 'em if You Got 'em

After eight steps of intervention, a backrub and some Steely Dan, a good cigarette break is always well deserved. If you don't smoke, this may be a good time to start.

While you are smoking, take the time to do a little inventory. Ask yourself the following questions: How many people in my group are still alive? Do the dead people have any cigarettes on them that we can bum? How about my friend the lycanthrope? Is he still eating anyone? Will he want one of our cigarettes when he's finished? Perhaps the survivors in the group should split the dead people's cigarettes after the werewolf has had his share?

11. Kill The '*Individual.*'

When therapists are in session they will sometimes recommend that a person kill the *individual* as in the *individual inside of himself.*

In other words, it's important to think about other people's needs instead of your own needs and put other people's needs first. In the werewolfing community this is not the case as it is recommended to kill the actual individual, like with a knife or large rock. You could squash him with a bulldozer, that works.

It is important to be thorough when killing the individual. Don't just shoot the thing once and walk away. That will always come back to haunt you. You have to squash the beast in a car crusher or blow it up with a gas pump or burn it to death on the electric lines in a brilliant fury of smoke and certain doom. Drowning in the ocean is a good one. Tie that individual to something heavy like an anchor and then anchors away.

Afterward, be sure to hug and kiss your new love interest now that the two of you are positive the werewolf is dead.

12. Final Step—Self Realization

Self Realization is where you and your new love interest realize that even though you shot the werewolf five times, smashed it in the car crusher, blew it up on the electric lines and sank it with the Titanic to the bottom of the icy sea . . . somehow . . . that werewolf is still alive.

Now kill it for real this time. You don't even have to do anything different. Kill the werewolf the same way you killed it the first time, but for some reason this time it will work! Now kiss your new love interest again and know it's . . . uh . . . really over.

CHAPTER 13
WINTER SIGHTINGS

The winter months in the U.P. host the largest volume of werewolf sightings for the entire year. Besides the large number of snowmo-werewolves, false sightings are the main factor contributing to the increase—a person thinks they see a werewolf but it's just something buried under the deep snow.

These false sightings are due to a sharp decline in temperature and a sharp rise in cabin fever. By mid-February in the U. P. the sun hasn't even been proven to exist. The longer and darker winter gets, and the more time people spend inside their cabins, the higher the likelihood of suffering from cabin fever and seeing a werewolf. Cabin fever is a syndrome of light deprivation where an individual begins to hallucinate and become moody. Below are some of the most famous false sightings in recent history.

FAMOUS FALSE SIGHTINGS

February 21, 1969

Believing they saw a werewolf during a blizzard, Bert and Tammy Scholander shoot nine silver bullets into a barbecue grill on their back porch. Shocked by a lack of blood and a flying temperature-control knob, they fail to remember the eggs they were boiling.

This results in the loss of their house by fire. During the fire, Bert thinks he sees another werewolf in his burning living room and empties his Smith and Wesson into his Lay-ze-boy recliner.

January 15, 1976

After two straight weeks of sub-zero temperatures and blowing snow, Roger McCoodle calls police to report his patio furniture as a family of werewolves with matching rod-iron weaves. After several questions, a moment of silence and some embarrassing backtracking, McCoodle attempts to save face by reporting that his neighbor cheated on his taxes and bought Cuban cigars. Years later, the trees in McCoodle's yard begin to die from unknown causes.

April 1, 1994

During a blizzard and whiteout, Richard Sklaarjiing calls 9-1-1 to report a large werewolf in his underpants. The following is a transcript of the call between The Dispatcher (DP) and Mr. Sklaarjiing (SK):

DP: "9-1-1?"
SK: "Ya, I'd like ta report a werewolf."

DP: "Did you say a werewolf?"

SK: "Oh ya, dere's a werewolf in my underpants."

DP: "In your underpants? Sir did you say there is a werewolf in your underpants?"

SK: "You betchya. What're you gonna do about it?"

DP: "What am I going to do about it?"

SK: "Yup. What 're you gonna do about dat werewolf in my underpants?"

DP: "Oh my God."

SK: "You like dat werewolf in my underpants, don't ya?"

DP: "Sir . . . this is . . . illegal."

SK: "Mary it's me, the Chief. I'm just kidding. April fools!"

DP" "Oh my God!"

SK: "Gotchya, didn't I?"

DP: "Yes! I thought you were some crazy guy. Oh my God I thought you were serious!"

SK: "Yeah, uh—actually I was pretty serious about that werewolf in my pants stuff."

DP: "Uh . . ."

March 12, 1987

After a brutal four-month stretch of cloud-cover and a March blizzard, the elderly Betsy-Ann Laborsludge fires her dead husband's Civil War Replica rifle at her next-door neighbor's log-splitter, thinking it's a werewolf. She destroys the twelve-horsepower Briggs and Stratton gasoline engine and any hopes that the occupant, Mr. Delbert Gribbs will become her newest suitor.

Numerous apologetic attempts via baked goods and sweets produce no results, so Mrs. Laborsludge shoots his lawnmower too, saying, "I thought it was another werewolf, Deadbeat."

October 14, 2005

After an early October blizzard, Gerald Morganweiss, a transplant from South Florida, panics when he loses sight of his bird feeder. He spends the next seven days calling various places of business inquiring as to what he should do about all of the white stuff.

After learning that it is snow and the upcoming winter may be as long as six months, Morganweiss retreats to his study to watch old reruns of *The Outer Limits*. In March, he threatens to shoot his landlord after claiming his landlord is a werewolf. In July, he uses his landlord as a reference on a credit application. He later regrets this decision.

Winter, 2007

Perhaps the most famous false sighting was reported in the winter of 2007, via the diary of Eldmar Skandersun, a retiree from Escanaba:

During the blizzard of January 22, 23, and 24th, I saw a large black werewolf lurking next to my woodpile in the back yard. I was terrified so I called to my wife in the other room.

"Honey, there's a werewolf in the back yard!"

"*Come in here,*" *she said, "I'm watching a western.*"

I ran back to the kitchen window and looked out to the back yard again. The wind was howling and the snow was piling up. We had been inside our cabin for eight weeks without sunlight and I couldn't believe my eyes. The werewolf was massive.

"*Honey! It's right there—a giant werewolf hunched down next to our woodpile!*"

"*Quit looking out that window,*" *she said.*

I took another sip of my beer and gave the beast a good hard look. It had buried itself under the snow to escape the heavy blizzard. The snow had piled up all around the thing except for the top of its head. It was shiny and black, almost flat at times, swaying in the hard wind.

I couldn't believe it. For six U.P. winters I had longed to see a werewolf up close and now one of them was right in front of me in the back yard.

"*Bring me a beer!*" *said my wife from the other room.*

"*I can't, I'm watching this werewolf!*"

"*Quit staring out that window and bring me a beer!*"

When I returned to the kitchen again I looked out the window and the werewolf was still there, evil and sullen, crouching next to the log pile under the snow and wind, the darkness enveloping every moment of its life. The howl of the thing almost sounded like the wind whistling against the side of our cabin, but I was sure it was a werewolf.

"Quit staring out that window and get in here!" yelled my wife. "Glenn Ford just beat up three people."

"There's a werewolf in the back yard!"

"I'm watching the movie!"

"You're the one who started the conversation," I said.

"Because you won't stop staring out that window, now get in here!"

I went back into the living room and watched the movie with my wife, but all I could think about was the werewolf lurking by the woodpile. The movie was Jubal, directed by Delmar Daves. It was a 1956 film, staring Glenn Ford, Earnest Borgnine, Rod Steiger and Valerie French. I didn't really watch the film but I think it was about love, lust, and betrayal on a cattle ranch, confronting a man running from his past—not sure. The only thing I could think about was the werewolf in our back yard.

The next day about noon, I looked outside to see if there were any tracks or dead bodies. They were gone. The snow had been falling non-stop for weeks and covered up the evidence. The only thing I found was fresh snow. Even if there had been dead bodies around, there was so much fresh snow they would have been undetectable.

I examined the woodpile where I had seen the werewolf hunching over, but there was nothing there, just our barbecue grill covered in heavy snow except for an exposed piece of the black plastic cover.

There were no werewolf tracks leading to or from the grill so I decided to wait and see if the beast would return again that night. After sundown, the snow and wind continued to pound our cabin.

My wife and I were having beers and watching Firecreek. I think it was a 1968 film directed by Vincent McEveety. It starred Jimmy Stewart, Henry Fonda and Inger Stevens. A remorseful gunman fights a sheriff who won't back down to save his small town—not sure, didn't really watch. I was too obsessed with the werewolf.

I decided to sneak into the kitchen and look out to the back yard. Sure enough, the werewolf was back, hunched in the backyard under heavy snow except for part of his head, blowing in the hard wind.

"It's back! The werewolf is back!"

"Quit looking out that window!" said my wife. "Jimmy Stewart is wrapping his bullet wound. He's going to try to kill all three of them!"

It was a terrifying and fitful night. I couldn't sleep knowing that werewolf was in our back yard, so the next day I went out to try and kill it. Sadly it was the same situation—too much fresh snow for tracks to be visible. I decided to keep an eye out that window all winter in case it came back.

And it did.

Every night for two months that werewolf lived and moved right next to our woodpile. And every night I would take a quick peek out the window to make sure it was still there, and every night there it was, huddling next to the log pile under the snow, right where the barbecue grill should have been.

"I'm going to kill that werewolf!" I said to my wife.

"Quit looking out that window. It's cabin fever."

Then something remarkable happened in late March. The snow melted and the werewolf just up and left. It was the end of a remarkable experience. Not only did I get to see a werewolf, I got to see one every night for most of February and March. I even came up with a name for him—"The Polite Werewolf," because every day he would re-set our barbecue grill in the same spot under the snow where he had been hiding the night before. He even took the time to replace the black plastic cover underneath all of that snow.

Maybe next year the werewolf will return and I'll watch Sabata. It's a 1969 film directed by Gianfranco Perillini. It stars Lee Van Cleef, William Berger, Linda Veras and Ignazio Spallas.

I think it's the story of a post-civil-war gunfighter who wheels and deals at the Mexican border against a town of corrupt officials and competing desperados—in Technicolor—not sure, haven't seen it.

CHAPTER 14
OTHER HOT SPOTS

Michigan is a werewolf watcher's paradise. You can walk along the shore of any Great Lake and catch a glimpse of slow-changers or fast-changers, or you can traverse the meadows and forests looking for limbs and other remains of previous watchers who called Michigan *home*. For many Michigan werewolfers, summer is a delight as the state hosts thousands of migrating werewolves returning from Florida. If you're planning a werewolfing trip, here are several places where you can catch werewolves in action.

The Porcupine Mountains Wilderness State Park

The Porcupine Mountains Wilderness State Park is a recreational werewolf haven. On the south shore of Lake Superior in Michigan's Upper Peninsula, this park boasts 60,000 acres of werewolf bliss. Walk on the trails through the forest and you're likely to see all types of Lycanthropes—grey, black, brown or close-up.

Lucky visitors to this park have seen werewolves so close that when it was all over, they had nothing left to wave goodbye with. The park is also popular with back packers, and many a throat-ripping has occurred along this secluded trail. Look for bloody pieces of t-shirt, backpack, and other clothing in the leaves on either side of the trail.

The Au Train Werewolf Trail

If you're on the hunt for popular werewolves you'll want to follow the Au Train Werewolf Trail. Located near the Au Train Campground, this interpretive three-mile walk is ideal for novice werewolfers. In May and June, over twenty varieties of werewolves have been spotted along the trail.

The Au Train Werewolf Trail leads through uplands, forest, and bog to an observation platform that overlooks Au Train Lake and its surrounding wetlands. This platform created by DNRE officials who were last seen in July 2003. Particularly impressive is the visible bone-yard complete with forest ranger hats.

Whitefish Point

Whitefish Point is a jack pine-covered dune peninsula surrounded by the waters of Lake Superior. During the summer, this peninsula becomes a haven for werewolves returning from Florida. That's why werewolfers, werewolf hunters and possibly vampires and homicidal robots frequent the area. It is located near Paradise Michigan—made famous in the novel *A Cold Day in Paradise*, by Steve Hamilton, a suspected werewolf.

When the weather gets colder, that's when the real show begins. The DNRE once estimated that between 5,000 and 10,000 werewolves migrated through the area every year. Most were shot or never heard from again. Don't be surprised if you see a werewolf peeing in public right in front of you, and of course, drinking domestic light beer. Who knows if he'll attack when he's finished?

St. Ignace

Since St. Ignace is one of the oldest European cities in Michigan, it stands to reason that it is also a great place to do a little werewolfing. St. Ignace is located at the northern end of the Mackinac Bridge, and south of the bridge is Mackinaw City. No one knows why the words Mackinac and Mackinaw are spelled differently, but pronounced the same. This author suspects werewolves are to blame.

The St. Ignace Mission

The St. Ignace Mission is now a municipal park. It was the site of a mission established by Father Père Jacques Marquette. Father Marquette is the French Jesuit Priest who founded Sault St. Marie and later St. Ignace. No one is sure if Father Marquette used the church to watch werewolves, but we found this quote in one of his writings: "What stinks in here?"

Later, in 1677, the St. Ignace Mission became the site of Father Marquette's grave. Although he officially died at the age of 38 from dysentery, Lycanthropy has not been ruled out. A second mission was established at a different site in 1837 and moved here in 1954 in order to fool any other possible werewolves.

Most travelers to the Straits area will be making the visit to Mackinac Island one of their top priorities. Although it is difficult to see werewolves ON the island of Mackinac, werewolves are visible from just *off* the island.

Stand in the water up to your knees and look back toward shore. Now raise one leg while holding one finger on your nose and place your left hand on top of your head. Repeat this chant over and over:

"Ayma-reeall-dome-arse, ayma-reeall-dome-arse."

People around you may snicker and snap photos. Simply disregard these people, as they do not have access to your level of technical information.

Sault St. Marie

The Soo as it's referred to, was founded by Father Marquette, one of the first Europeans to explore the region, but only with the help of the Native Americans. In fact, he didn't explore the region at all. It was more like a guided canoe tour. *The Soo* is one of the only places to see both Native American and Canadian werewolves.

Tahquamenon Falls

Tahquamenon River was made famous in the Longfellow poem *Hiawatha*. According to Indian legend, the name can be attributed to the water's amber color, the result of the leaching of tannic acid from nearby swamps. This has been directly attributed to werewolves as werewolves drink DLB and pee tannic acid.

One little known fact is that the falls are the second largest falls east of the Mississippi River, the largest being Niagara Falls. In Niagara, werewolves will sometimes plunge over the falls in barrels. In Tahquamenon, most werewolves just hang out at the brewery

The Ojibwa tribe of Algonquin Indians used the Tahquamenon River primarily for trading beaver and werewolf fur. When white settlers took over, they used the river to float logs at their famous logging camp—camp #33, the number of werewolf casualties in the camp.

Copper Harbor

Copper Harbor is in the western U.P. about an hour's drive north of the city of Houghton. Copper was first mined in this area by an ancient vanished race of werewolves between 5,000 and 1,200 BC.

These ancient lycanthropes worked the copper-bearing rock by using fire and cold water to break the copper ore into smaller pieces from which they could extract the metal with hand-held hammering stones or stone hatchets. With this copper, they made a big still out in the woods.

Scientists and engineers estimate that it would have required 10,000 men 1,000 years to develop the extensive operations carried on throughout the region. However, you and I know that werewolves are capable of doing the work of thousands

Although no artifacts were found, they did find twelve cans of domestic light beer and a bag of pork-rinds. Also, these were later determined to belong to one of the researchers.

Manistique

Manistique was founded in 1871, by Henry R. Schoolcraft. Schoolcraft named it after the Ojibwa word *Mon*istique, for the cinnamon color of the river, but when registered with the state, an error in spelling was made because Henry Schoolcraft was a werewolf and everyone knows that werewolves can't spell.

Today, the Manistique area is where sightings of the infamous Dog-man have occurred. The Dog-man is a wild-dog type of man who runs around the area on nights when the moon is full. Although referred to as the Dog-man, this individual is believed to be a werewolf descendent of Henry R. Schoolcraft. Evidence of this came to light one day when a group of teenagers saw the

Dog-man. The Dog-man howled and said, "Hey, you teenagers, I'm a werewolf descendent of Henry R. Schoolcraft. Shouldn't you kids be in school? I need a note from your parents! They were eaten before they could hand him their notes.

Menominee

Menominee gets its name from a regional Native American tribe called the Menominee, which, loosely translated means *Wild Rice*. After the arrival of European settlers, the name of the town was changed to *Combo Platter*, which loosely translated means an 8 oz. grilled sirloin, vegetable medley, and choice of potato. Due to the limited amount of space on a postal envelope, several humans were sacrificed and the name was changed back to Menominee.

The first werewolf to arrive in Menominee was a man named Marshal Burns Lloyd, owner of Lloyd manufacturing. In 1917, Lloyd invented a loom that could weave wicker baby buggies together. Lloyd, who loved to feast on children, began manufacturing all kinds of wicker products including furniture.

Lloyd was eaten by another werewolf, Bill Crapp, the owner of the local brewery when Lloyd talked Crapp into making his beer bottles out of wicker. Crapp went bankrupt when all the beer ran out of the wicker bottles.

The Pictured Rocks

The Lake Superior coastline in Alger County can be considered some of the best werewolf watching in the Great Lakes area. Host to Pictured Rocks National Lakeshore, Alger County features beautiful scenery and a good chance of spotting a supernatural beast.

You can kayak or hike the shoreline or see werewolves on the cliffs by tour boat. There are also plenty of rivers, streams and entrails that offer a great atmosphere for winter snowmobiling or summertime gore.

Alger County is named for Russell Alger, then governor of Michigan. Alger was a known werewolf who attempted to get the state legislature to make June 13th Pork Fat Day. He was unsuccessful in this venture, but he did manage to eat several of the people who voted against his idea.

Later, Alger left office and disappeared into the wilderness around Munising, MI. To this day, snowmobilers claim to occasionally see a werewolf wearing a top hat and monocle.

Mines and Werewolf Towns

Mines and werewolf towns offer some of the best werewolfing in the Upper Peninsula. All that remains are a few old mine shafts, some deserted hundred-year-old houses, and a number of unholy bone yards.

These are the types of areas where werewolves love to hang out. Adolescent werewolves will use these areas to have a bush party with a bon-fire and beer and a lot of other werewolf-related activity.

Villages were built at the site of the mines and were known as horror settings, whereas the mines were known as hellholes of death. Today, some locations have a few people living in the area, but most of the old mining houses are only used as an annual hideout from the carnivorous curse left behind

Conditions for werewolves in the late 1800's and early 1900's were tough and these men, women and children were strong, courageous and delicious. Winters were long and hard. Supplies were brought in by boat and had to last all winter. Conveniences were few, but these people from all over the world established homes, churches, schools, and provided werewolves with some of the whitest meat Europe had to offer.

Central Mine

In 1854, The Central Mine was given an award for safety and a sign was posted that read: Number of days since last throat ripping—03.

Located in an ancient mining pit along an outcrop below Greenstone Bluff, Cornish werewolves and their families flocked from Britain and with their extensive mining knowledge helped make this a successful venture.

It also led to a new North England—Scandinavian mix of werewolf known as Yahoos.

Cliff Mine

Established in 1844 by John Hayes, a werewolf from Pittsburgh, PA, Cliff Mine was the first profitable mine in the Keweenaw. The mine employed 840 men. Although 802 of them were eaten, great copper masses were found despite these setbacks. One hundred tons of copper was pulled out of the cliff mine, an amount that could be carried by three or four well-fed werewolves.

The Cliff Mine closed in 1873, after Hayes ate the last employee. Today, little remains except some old foundations, some rock piles and the occasional re-emergence of an ancient curse.

Delaware

The Delaware Mine opened in 1874, but no one would work there because a werewolf was found to be hiding inside.

Gay

The village of Gay is hilarious. A few miles east of Kersearge, on the east shore of the Keweenaw Peninsula, Gay has been made light of more than any single town in the Upper Peninsula. People from all over the world travel to Gay and attempt to make a joke that locals haven't already heard.

Mandan

If you are interested in seeing a realistic werewolf town, your trip is not complete without a drive through Mandan. This was the site of the Mandan Mining Company

(1863) and was home at one time to several werewolves. Today, people can experience the same boredom experienced by the original three hundred residents.

Phoenix

The Phoenix Mine proves that early miners had little to no sense of geography.

Quincy Mine Smelter

The Quincy Mine Smelter is the only remaining smelter in the Lake Superior region. Smelters are a great way to keep any conversation lively.

"Hey did you hear about all the smelting that went on at that smelter?"

Or,
"He who smelt it dealt it,"
Or,
"We should name our heavy metal band Smelter."

Old Victoria

One of the first sites ever mined for copper in Old Victoria is located near Rockland, MI, a notorious hang out for werewolves. The famous Ontonagon Werewolf was discovered here in the Ontonagon River Valley. In addition to the Finns, other werewolves in the area were Croatian, Austrian, Italian, Canadian, Swedish, and some guy from New Jersey.

CHAPTER 15
ANATOMY OF A WEREWOLF

The werewolf digestive system is much like a modern in-sink-erator. Filled with mustard gas, Chinese peppers, chlorine bleach and Spam, the stomach of a werewolf can digest just about any human.

Several times throughout history werewolf stomachs have been cut open only to reveal a number of people, a rubber boot and a license plate. Upper Peninsula werewolves have indiscriminate stomachs as they have been raised on cheese-curds, DLB, homemade venison sausage, hot dogs, cocktail weenies, potato sausage, polish sausage, bratwurst, sausage gravy over biscuits, breakfast sausage and of course—summer sausage.

In Calumet, Michigan, a famous werewolf named Erskel Raiijjiicckk once ate an entire octopus on fish fry Friday. Raiijjiicckk was rumored to have his octopus flown in fresh every Thursday night from a Japanese whaling vessel via a connection in Finland. No information is available on what he ate the other six nights of the week.

Werewolves are hungry, dangerous, supernatural creatures who have a long, thick, furry coat that protects them from the cold. Both male and female werewolves have beards and some have pointed black horns. Female werewolves have udders from which werewolf milk is extracted.

The Werewolf Digestive System

Below (Figure 3.) is a diagram of the internal digestive system of a Werewolf. It shows the four stomach chambers and the intestines as well as a small garbage disposal.

Mature werewolves have digestive tracts that are similar to those of cattle and consist of the mouth, four stomach compartments and intestines. Unlike cattle, werewolves have extra incisors or canine teeth. Werewolves don't depend on the hard palate, they use their sharp lower incisor teeth, lips and tongue to take limbs from people and shove them into their mouths.

Unlike Vampires (not proven to exist), werewolves do not drink blood; they eat flesh. Blood is just a bonus.

Figure 3. Werewolf Digestive System

The Werewolf Stomach

Shagbox.

This is the largest of the four stomach compartments of werewolves. The capacity of the werewolf's shagbox ranges from three to six gallons depending on the person he ate.

Mule Housing

This compartment contains many microorganisms that breakdown potato sausage, ground foods and delivery people.

The conversion of the pork or human parts to fatty acids is the result of microbiological activities in the Mule Housing. These fatty acids are absorbed through the Mule Housing walls and provide up to 80 percent of the total energy requirements of most supernatural creatures.

Werewolf microorganisms also convert components of people to useful products such as belches, saliva, the Bcomplex vitamins, and a blood-curdling howl. Finally, the microorganisms themselves are digested further in the digestive tract and emerge as a powerful wind.

Breadbox.

This compartment, also known as the hardware stomach or bubble-stump, is located just below the entrance of the esophagus into the stomach. The capacity of the Breadbox of werewolves ranges from 25 to 50 gallons of human chum.

Omygod.

This compartment, also known as the stuffer, consists of many folds or layers of tissue that grind up people and remove most of the water. The capacity of the Omygod in werewolves is approximately 65 gallons or 2-3 dozen children.

Rearbox.

This compartment is more often considered the true stomach of werewolves. It functions like a human stomach. It contains hydrochloric acid and digestive enzymes that breakdown food particles before they enter the small intestine. The capacity of the Rearbox can hold upwards of two small villages.

Werewolves aren't particular about who they eat, but they will not consume food that contains any health benefit. Werewolves require a large volume of food and will eat a wide variety of people regardless of age, race, religion, creed or sexual orientation.

Werewolves will eat young people as well as old. They also like bark from trees. Werewolves are inquisitive and will nibble and investigate most limbs and throats before they eat them. However, most attacks come without warning

One reason we love to watch werewolves is that they give us so many reasons to feel superior. Much of what they do is so unfathomable we can't help but wonder what they're thinking. Will that thing eat us? We wonder.

CHAPTER 16
WEREWOLVES IN SPACE

The Theoretical Physics of Lycanthropy

Wofler's Principle states: If a person infected with Lycanthropy travels into space, he will always be a werewolf, because in space the moon is always full. If the werewolf retains a relative position of orbit with the moon, this will continue for eternity or until he eats the remainder of the crew aboard his ship.

If a werewolf travels at the speed of light away from the moon, he will change back into a human because the light reflected by the moon will be unable to reach the traveling werewolf. Also, at any speed, a werewolf can change back into a person as soon as he travels out of the moon's glow.

As the werewolf passes the moons of other planets, he will be subjected to whatever disease is caused by those planet's moons. For example, one of Jupiter's moons is called Europa. This moon causes Europism, a disease where Americans are turned into Europeans. The traveling werewolf will immediately complain about poor quality wine, levy excessive taxes and demand a single currency for all of its neighboring nations. Jupiter in fact, has sixty-three moons. Imagine the high cost of living!

Any space-traveling werewolf will be subjected to any disease caused by these moons as long he maintains a relative position to these moons. When he passes in view of these moons he will change back into a human as the light reflected can't reach him. Therefore, any infected individual who intends to travel through space should pack a lot of extra clothing. If you cannot afford suitcases you can make your own with duct tape.

The *Space-Time Werewolf Continuum Principle* states that if the earth's moon causes Lycanthropy, it stands to reason that somewhere on some distant earth-like planet, the opposite is also true. Instead of the moon changing people into werewolves, their moon would change wolves into werepeople. Rather than a human on two legs morphing into a four-legged howling creature, on that planet a four-legged wolf would turn into a two-legged talking creature. These creatures would then spend full-moon nights barhopping and trying to impress younger, more attractive changelings, and lying about how successful they are.

Physicists believe that any possible werewolf condition is possible in space.

There also may be parallel universes where everyone is a werewolf except for a few regular humans. The humans would eat the werewolves, ride snowmobiles, and consume excess quantities of domestic light beer. Food for thought.

CHAPTER 17
ENVIRONMENTAL IMPACT OF WEREWOLVES

As green science and technology improve, the werewolf question has become more important. I was asked a while ago if I could provide some information on werewolf impact on the environment. Here is what I came up with.

Food Production

Each year, the United States produces about 10% of the world's werewolves but consumes about 26% of the world's total production of werewolf-loving food.

The Midwest is the largest producer of werewolves and consumes about 43% of the total production of domestic light beer, pork sausage, cheese, and Ranch dressing. Let's not forget the corn chips.

Overall, the U.P. consumes about 16% of the total amount of werewolf-loving food consumed in the U.S., but produces only 5% of the werewolf food supply. That's because werewolves can feed off of a seasonal supply of non-residents.

Air Pollution

Although great strides have been made over the past thirty years to reduce air pollution from werewolves' farts and burps, gasses on public and private land still account for a significant proportion of air pollution worldwide.

This is because the number of werewolves in the past thirty years has increased by more than ten times, although there is no specific evidence confirming this fact.

Water Pollution

There are a number of ways that werewolves contribute to water pollution:

Pee.

The effect of runoff deposited from meat particles, bodily fluids, and ingested chemicals from convenience stores is difficult to quantify, but a 2006 survey of 693,905 river-miles in werewolf country estimated that werewolf runoff was the leading source of impairment for at least 13% of the river-miles.

One EPA researcher estimated the amount of werewolf runoff from public land to be in the hundreds of thousands of tons per year. He was never heard from again.

Sweat.

Werewolf sweat really stinks it up. A recent survey was interrupted because it stunk so bad. Survey takers could not complete their survey forms.

Leaky werewolf septic tanks.

As of 1998, there were approximately 92,000 suspected werewolf septic tanks in the US, mostly in the Midwest. A cumulative total of 50,000 tanks had been pumped, with confirmed leaks from 10,000 werewolf tanks. This is because werewolves are too lazy to contact a certified professional for tank maintenance, and when a certified professional does show up, they eat him.

Werewolf Droppings.

One quart of werewolf droppings can contaminate a million gallons of fresh water. The EPA estimates 13.4% of all werewolf dung is illegally dumped, while another

10.1% is smelled and/or ridiculed. This has little environmental impact, but is kind of funny.

Noise Pollution

Werewolf farts have become perhaps the primary source of noise pollution in the Great Lake's area. A Federal Smell Administration (FSA) brochure states that a typical werewolf fart going 50 mph is twenty times as loud as a tractor trailer, and eight times as loud as the Space Shuttle. It's also six hundred and forty times as loud as The Edgar Winter Band.

The Organization for Olfactory Cooperation and Development (OOCD) estimated in 2009 that 37 percent of the U.S. population was exposed to annoying levels of werewolf gas (greater than 55 decibels), while 7% was exposed to levels that made conversation difficult. For example:

"I think we should go to lunch."

"What? I can't hear you because of that god-awful werewolf gas!"

"Is that gas? I thought it was The Edgar Winter Band."

Land Use

Werewolves require a lot of space. In urban areas, werewolves tend to get a lot of jaywalking tickets, but ticket-writing beat cops are disposed of without warning.

In 2010, rural roads covered an estimated 13,363 square miles of land, an area larger than the state of Maryland. After discovering this, werewolves attacked people on an additional 4,012 square miles of land, an area larger than Delaware. It's possible that werewolves could eat everyone in Delaware.

Solid Waste

Over one thousand werewolves were shot by silver bullets in 2010. About 75% of the dead werewolves were burned so no one would ask questions, while the remaining 25% were sent to secret government laboratories for experimentation and production of a secret werewolf army. In that same year, an estimated 200 million aluminum beer cans left over from dead werewolves were scrapped, 76% of which were recovered and recycled.

The 63 million beer cans that were not recovered were dumped, adding to the approximately 800 million beer cans currently stockpiled in dumps around the country. These werewolf can-dumps, classified as an ongoing environmental hazard, are ideal breeding grounds for young werewolves who love to suck on empty beer cans.

If you shoot and kill a werewolf, please recycle werewolf beer cans or report it to your nearest secret laboratory.

Effects on Wildlife

The primary way werewolves kill wildlife is not by hunting or trapping, but with their breath. It is estimated that werewolf breath kills over a million animals in *exhalations* every year in the U.S.

Our Responsibility

As werewolf watchers, it is up to us to report any ecologically damaging werewolf. Also, please contact authorities to report current werewolf stats and sightings that you may have. Use caution when doing this as local authorities may deem you *crazy*, or give you some type of code number like 165, which is basically cop talk for "Don't listen to that guy, he's crazy."

It is truly sad that in this day and age werewolves are still misunderstood. Except for the eating-people thing, which is understood quite well, we hope to learn much more about these terrific creatures in the future.

CHAPTER 18
A DAY IN THE LIFE OF A
WEREWOLFER

It's six-thirty in the morning and my Sherpa is taking me on the hunt of a lifetime. We're not deep in the woods or hiking one of the rolling mountains of The Porcupines, we're in Bruce Crossing, Michigan, on the western side of the U.P.

Arjj, my Sherpa, has a side garden full of carrots, sunflowers, green beans and other delicious vegetables that we're using to drape ourselves for the day's werewolf watch.

"Tie these mammoth sunflowers to your body for protection," says Arjj. "Werewolves hate sunflowers."

It's the experience of a lifetime and I'm eager to gather every piece of information I can.

"Why do they hate the sunflowers?" I ask.

Arjj is up on his tiptoes, thumbing through the variety of mammoths.

"Because they're sunny," he jokes.

I almost fall for it, but he gives me a smile.

"The seeds are healthy," he says, "Healthy foods repel werewolves. Tie those carrots to your feet."

"To my feet?"

"Yeah, it masks your scent. I knew this guy once who put rutabagas in small burlap sacks then strapped them under his armpits."

"Did it work?"

"No, he was eaten."

Arjj is squatting down in the garden like he's been farming for decades. He is unfazed by the possibility of death.

"We use carrots, sunflowers and snow peas. They're sweeter than rutabagas."

I lend Arjj a hand with some of the tougher snow peas and the conversation turns toward our backgrounds.

"How many werewolves have you seen, Arjj?"

"None yet, you?"

"I almost saw one in my backyard," I say. I look to the back of the garden. "What's with that corn over there?"

"Its feed corn. I think werewolves like it 'cause it's been chewed in the back. There are some tracks over there."

I make my way to the chewed corn and look at the tracks.

"These look like deer tracks," I say.

Arjj gets an inquisitive look.

"Are you sure? How do you know?"

"They're hooves."

"Oh."

"How long have you been a Sherpa, Arjj?"

"How long have you been one, Dale?"

"I'm not one."

"That's right. Now shut up and tie those 'effing carrots to your feet."

He makes a convincing argument, so I tie the carrots around my feet and we head out to the forest. It spreads out before us and we hike on, looking like two vegetable sampler platters. The only thing missing is a side of ranch dressing and a doily.

The forests of the U.P. are old and mysterious. This particular patch is in the middle of a farming neighborhood cut out of Ottawa National Forest. I ask Arjj about some of the more popular U.P. tourist attractions I've read about.

"What about this Mystery Spot I see signs for?"

"It's a hangout for werewolves on the other side of Hiawatha. In the early 1950's, three surveyors stumbled across an area of land about 300 feet in diameter where their surveying equipment malfunctioned. The surveyors were also constantly light headed."

"From werewolf encounters?"

"No, they were drunk."

Arjj is leading me through some of the thicker thorn apples and cedar.

"Millions of people visit The Mystery Spot and some are eaten by werewolves. Most aren't. There's a theory that the guy who owns the place is a werewolf and he gets tourists to come by just so he can eat them. Afterwards, he steals their money to pay for his domestic light beer. Either way, the spot really is weird.

"Is he really a werewolf?"

"No, he's just some old guy."

"What types of things happen out there?"

Arjj pushes back some tree branches.

"A tall person may seem smaller by comparison. Also, you can climb a wall and tilt into the air without falling. There's also a maze, mini golf, game arcade, and souvenir gift shop."

"Do you work at The Mystery Spot?"

"Part-time."

We trudge further into the forest, draped in vegetables and sunflowers.

"What's this Paulding Light I hear about?"

"It's a ghost light that appears in Paulding, about fifteen miles from here."

"Are there werewolves there?"

"Huge ones."

"Shouldn't we be looking for werewolves over there?"

"That's a good question. You're starting to annoy me."

I kill the Q&A and we hike for the next three miles. The forest is beautiful and creepy. The silence is killing me, so I ask more stupid questions.

"Hey Arjj," I say.

"What?"

"See any werewolves yet?"

"Shhh! I think I see something."

I can't believe it. I was just joking around and now Arjj sees something.

"What is it?" I whisper.

"I think it's a large Brown werewolf."

"Holy crap!"

Arjj motions for me to stay quiet, but he sneezes and is suddenly yanked through the thicket. After a flurry of screaming and tearing sounds, I decide to head back to home base, leaving my guide behind. I run full speed back to the cabin.

Back at the cabin I wait for Arjj but it's getting late. A familiar sound in the back yard draws me to the window. I see a large bear cruising the property, digging up carrots and snapping up garden peas. I watch as he wanders away with an arm in his mouth similar to Arjj's.

My guide never returns so I decide to hold a small ceremony in the back yard. I burn the sunflowers and other vegetables that we tied to our feet. I don't know what else to do so I go back inside and play some Bob Dylan, drink some domestic light beer and have a small, improvised funeral. I didn't see a werewolf, but I take comfort in the fact that maybe Arjj did.

The next day I head over to The Mystery Spot and apply for his vacant part-time job.

CHAPTER 19
SELF-TEST

The world is full of werewolves and other vertebrates with painful, sometimes deadly bites. What you don't know about werewolves could hurt you. Take the following quiz to see how wise you are regarding Lycanthropes, the diseases they spread, and methods for avoiding and treating their bites.

    1.   Which one of the following Lycanthropes does not attack by cutting or piercing with its mouthparts?

A) Slow Changers
B) Fast Changers
C) The kind that look like Santa Claus
D) They all do

2. Finish this sentence—Werewolves . . .

A) . . . may kill you.
B) . . . probably will kill you.
C) . . . may probably kill you.

3. When werewolves bite, they cut through skin with their knife-like mouthparts. To avoid this:

A) Run.
B) Run faster.
C) Run as fast as you can.
D) Hoof and Mouth Disease.

4. Various chemical compounds are applied to skin or clothing to discourage werewolves. For example, the most effective repellents for werewolves can contain carrot

juice and turnip greens. What else discourages werewolves?

A) Citronella
B) Roundup
C) Not allowing him to see your blood-engorged throat.

5. Tiny werewolves known as wolfies can be an even greater nuisance in some areas because their bite is like the jab of a javelin and they can enter dwellings through ordinary doors. What is the common name for this group of werewolves?

A) Tinywolves.
B) Midgewolves
C) Frank, my neighbor

6. Medical experts often recommend a simple home treatment to help relieve the discomfort from werewolf bites. What is it?

A) Lemon Juice
B) Meat tenderizer.

C) Vinegar.
D) A small improvised funeral.

7. Which of the following statements about werewolves is true?

A) They are attracted by shiny surfaces.
B) They are most active on overcast days.
C) There's a werewolf behind you right now.

8. The world's most deadly werewolf is the:

A) Lockhorn Werewolf
B) Red Werewolf
C) The one that is behind you right now.

Quiz answers

1 D)
2-8 C)

Using What We Know

This practice test will help you with your decision-making.

1. You are in the woods alone. The moon is full. You hear the howl of a werewolf near you. You should:

A) Grab your binoculars.
B) Run for cover.
C) Eat a sandwich.

2. You've attempted to bait a werewolf with raw chicken but none have arrived. You should:

A) Sit tight. Keep waiting.
B) Yell very loudly, "Hey werewolves, where the crap are you?"
C) Eat the raw chicken

3. You suspect that your neighbor is a werewolf. He stops by to borrow your lawnmower. You should:

A) Give him the mower.
B) Confront him by saying, "Hey! I know you're a werewolf, you stinkin' fur-beast."
C) Hit him over the head with a shovel.
D) See if you can borrow some duct tape.

4. During the family dinner, Dad lets a really big one rip at the table. You should:

A) Keep eating. Pretend you didn't hear anything.
B) Cry out, "Holy crap, Dad. What a werewolf fart!"
C) Shoot him with a silver bullet.

5. You meet a new love interest and they turn out to be hairier than you originally suspected. You should:

A) Pretend you're with someone you really like, at least for the time being.

B) Say, "Whoa, shave much?"

C) Offer them a bucket of turkey guts.

6. You think you see a werewolf coming towards you, you should:

A) Sacrifice friends and family as a distraction.

B) Flail around like a wounded animal.

C) Wet your pants.

7. You're out for a day of werewolfing. Which of the following choices would make a better protective shed.

A) A cabin.

B) An outhouse.

C) A five-gallon bucket.

8. When snowmobile season opens you should:

A) Ride that shizzle!

B) Pee your name in the snow.

C) Post signs around town warning of

werewolves.

Quiz answers

1 B)
2-8 A)

CHAPTER 20
THE FAKE ENDING

At the end of most horror stories there is often an attempt to fool the audience into thinking that the creature has been killed, even though we all know he hasn't been. Most of the time the creature is just knocked out, faking, or hiding. Later, the creature attacks the heroes again only to be killed for real this time.

But wait, according to the sequel, the creature wasn't even killed at that time either. The creature slithered away into the forest and survived with the help of one of those great minions I referred to earlier.

Minions are evil henchmen who for one reason or another love to help supernatural creatures commit horrific murder. It's getting harder and harder to be a supernatural creature these days without the help of minions.

"Minion, dress my wounds. Minion, hide me until I'm healthy. Minion, bring me home a Subway sandwich or the liver of a goat."

A number of esteemed Universities in the U.S. now offer minionships as part of their exorbitantly overpriced educational programs. Courses include Minion 101: Service and Loyalty, and Minion 210: Concepts in Assisted Homicide. It should be noted that most successful minions are eventually killed regardless of education.

Another method of becoming a minion is to start out with a werewolf for a number of years until your trust is gained and a minion position becomes available. You'll get paid to learn but you may have to start in the werewolf mailroom. Also, you may be eaten in the mailroom.

Understanding the fake ending of books or movies is an important step in completing your werewolf-watching program. Werewolves move lighting fast and your time to make decisions will be limited. If you wish to watch werewolves with a number of your friends and/or your new love interest it is important that everyone be on the same page. When it feels as if the end is near, keep these fake-ending rules in mind.

After You

When a werewolf attacks, let someone else kill it first. Even if this person is successful you can rest assured the horrific beast is not really dead. After a brief period of celebration, the werewolf will come back to life and mutilate this individual. After this person is eaten, step in and kill the werewolf with whatever tool the dead person was using. For some reason, this time it will work.

Keep It Simple

No matter how grandiose the method of killing, the werewolf is not really dead. That means keep it simple—guns, knifes, magic spells, etc.

Unless you have access to a commercial trap door, planning an elaborate scheme to kill the werewolf is difficult and time consuming, and no matter what you do, the werewolf will not really be dead. Try shooting the werewolf from a distance with a silver bullet. After a brief celebration and resurrection, shoot him again.

Don't Forget The Minion

Don't ever forget the minion because he will burn you every time. A good minion working efficiently can help any homicidal creature resurrect for upwards of five sequels. Before you attempt to kill any werewolf attacking you, be sure and take care of his minion in advance. Minions can be found anywhere criminally insane people gather. Mental hospitals, your place of business, and The Federal Government are all good places to find minions.

Sacrifice

The best way to kill any beast over and over throughout any fake ending, is to spare yourself by baiting the werewolf with others in your party. This may seem unconventional, but in the worldwide werewolfing community this is commonplace. A nerdy kid with glasses works well, or people making love.

Werewolves will commonly attack these types of people first. Offering these people as sacrifices will give you time to let someone else kill the werewolf, have a brief celebration, wait for resurrection, and then kill it for real.

Strong Stomach

If you're going to do any type of advanced werewolfing, you'll have to get used to blood and gore. Finding the mutilated bodies of people you know is all part of observing these fascinating creatures.

If you come across the consumed carcass of someone you know, do not scream. This may alert werewolves in the area to your position. If you are at some type of social gathering, the werewolf may be in human form, disguised as one of your other friends. Simply return to the party. When someone asks you if everything is okay just say, "Yes."

If people begin disappearing and no bodies are found, there may be a minion at the party you have overlooked. With a keen eye, some discipline and good organization, any werewolfer can achieve success at the fake end.

CHAPTER 21
THE REAL ENDING

I'll say this, you and I have been through a lot together. If you can't remember what we've been through together, let me just remind you that we've been from Helsinki to the Soo and up to Houghton. We've studied the ways of werewolfing, the characteristics of these frightening beasts, and learned that things aren't always what they seem—especially when it comes to fake endings.

We've shared other emotions too. We've grown suspicious of one another and made light of the culture of beer drinking with remarkable casualness, regardless of the obvious health problems. I'm sure there were many, many more memorable moments that we shared together on our journey, I just can't remember any right now.

I want to thank you for participating in werewolf watching, one of the greatest up and coming activities expected to ever up and come. Also, remember to slouch down in your car seat and never be too sure that someone you meet isn't a werewolf—or *is* a werewolf—whichever way is easier for you to remember.

Again, don't be fooled by the fake ending and remember that you're now reading the real ending. The story isn't over until the fat lady gets her throat ripped out and a sequel is born.

Sequels

The basic problem with sequels is that they are packaged and sold to audiences on the premise of something new, but everyone knows sequels aren't new, they're just the same old story with a slightly different ending and maybe some younger characters.

Do this: tell a story to one of your friends. The next day, tell your friend the same story but with a slightly different ending. Do this a third, fourth, even a fifth time and see if your friend still speaks to you.

If someone did that to me, I would stop being friends after part two. If the person was a really good friend, there might be a part three, but only if they were a really good friend. Relatives don't count because you *have* to listen to their stories over and over again.

And now, the real ending:

BEERWOLF—The Eito Elchick Story

Eito stepped off the ship and past the porter in 1800's Sault Ste. Marie. The wooden plank to the dock was narrow and

Eito had to squeeze his chubby stomach past the porter. He had packed on the pounds during his long boat trip from Finland.

"Where's the crew?" asked the porter.

"I don't know. It's not like I ate them (burp)." Eito pointed out to the harbor. "Look, a ship in trouble!"

When the porter turned around to look, Eito snuck away.

Eito hit the road. He made his way to Houghton and found an alehouse to rest in. *Time to get drunk off of someone else's beer*, he thought.

Eito worked the crowd inside the alehouse. He stole a few sips of beer from several people. After four or five successful booze hawkings, Eito tried to steal a large swallow of beer from a miner at the end of the bar. As Eito swooped in, the miner saw him out of the corner of his eye.

"Hey you booze hawk, get out of my beer!"

"What do you mean?" said Eito.

The large miner stood chest to chest with Eito.

"I'm Brock Brunschweiger, the best miner in the U.P. territory and you were trying to booze-hawk some of my beer!"

"No I wasn't, I dropped . . . uh . . . my horse."

"I'm going to kick your Finnish butt!"

Eito thought for a moment.

"Is it a full moon tonight?"

"Yes it is," he said.

"Okay," said Eito. "I'll meet you out in front of this bar at midnight and we'll see whose butt gets kicked."

Just then a man of some authority stepped into the argument.

"I'm John Hayes, owner of The Cliffside Mine. Whichever one of you wins the fight tonight will not only have a job at the most prosperous mine in the U.P, you'll be my personal minion from this point forward."

Brock Brunschweiger faced Hayes. "I'm the best miner in this territory and I'm no man's minion!"

"Minion is the third highest paying job at the company."

"Like I said," said Brock, "I'm the best minion in this territory!"

Eito smiled and thought about the full moon that would be out later when he would become a shrieking hell-beast and obliterate Brunschweiger. He laughed to himself, thinking about the 840 miners and their families that were employed by the mine. If he could just get the minion job, he would be set for life. All he would need is a werewolf girlfriend who could help him eat upwards of 802 miners and their families.

Then Eito noticed Hayes had taken his eyes of his beer. Eito swooped in and scored a small swallow of beer from Hayes' mug before Hayes could turn back around. Brock saw him but didn't say anything to Hayes. Instead he pointed at Eito.

"I'm gonna' bust you up tonight," said Brock.

"Bring it on, tough guy."

Then Eito pointed toward Hayes. "Mr. Hayes wants you," said Eito.

When Brock turned toward Hayes, Eito picked up Brock's mug and chugged all of his beer.

Eito left the bar and hiked into the hills to wait for darkness. He could hear a loud holler from inside the tavern, the shriek of a man who just realized his beer had been stolen.

As he walked, Eito plotted his U.P. success. The fight would be his. The minion job would be his. Several free ales would also be his. Eito hiked further into the hills. He felt light headed and excited. This new land, The Upper Peninsula of Michigan, what a great place to steal people's ale, mine for copper, and of course, eat a number of unsuspecting locals.

He sauntered down the street in Houghton knowing that no matter how bad things got, at least he could kill some more people. The important thing now was to maintain a low profile until full moon

He continued toward downtown Houghton.

"Hiya, stranger," said a voice.

"What the heck?"

"I'm Mary," said the voice.

Eito looked to his right and there she was, the most beautiful girl in the world. Next to her was Mary, about a six or a seven, with a bottle of beer in her hand.

"I'm Eito," he replied.

The most beautiful girl in the world left, but Mary stayed behind. She licked her lips and took a big pull off her bottle of beer as she spoke to Eito.

"I heard about the fight tonight—you and Brunschweiger. I think fighting is hot."

"Oh yeah?"

"Yeah. I don't know what it is about you, fella, but I want some of what you got."

"Come along with me. After dark, I'll give you some of what I got."

Mary smiled.

"Look over there," said Eito.

When Mary looked, he grabbed her bottle of beer and chugged it. Mary looked back at him.

"Now I get why you're alone," she said.

"Don't worry about it, after tonight you won't ever go hungry again."

"What about thirsty?"

"You may want to watch your beverage around me."

Eito and Mary went up into the hills and drank some more beer. They looked at the village in the valley below as the sun went down and the full moon rose.

"Uh-oh," said Eito.

"What is it?" asked Mary.

It was too late. The transformation had begun. Eito's bones and muscles cracked and popped. His face began stretching and hair began popping up all over his body. He looked at Mary and pleaded with the last remaining shred of humanity in his voice—"Run!" he screamed.

"That is so hot!" said Mary. "I knew there was something about you!"

She lunged at Eito knocking him down and kissing his transforming body. For miles away, people could hear the howl, "Oooowwwwww!"

Then Eito howled as loud as Mary did, "Oooooowwwwww!"

Eito couldn't help it. At the most important time, he bit a chunk out of Mary's neck. She sat up and looked at him.

"You're one kinky devil!" she said.

Mary passed out. As she lay there, her neck magically began to heal. Eito hunched over her, checking on her progress.

"By the power vested in me," growled Eito, "I swear I will leave this woman here in the bushes to mend on her own while I go into town to beat the crap out of Brock Brunschweiger."

And he did.

Eito stalked toward town on furry, Finlander werewolf feet, hiking through the bushes, the rivers, streams, rocks and lawns. Several times he came across pedestrians but didn't eat them. He was saving his strength for some big time Brunschweiger. The minion job would be his. And then together, he and Mary would rule the U.P. territory, unless Mary wasn't in the bushes when he got back, in which case he would have to look around for someone else. But if he found someone else, then he could make this brilliant speech all over again, even though it wasn't a real speech, it was just a thought inside his head.

He continued to downtown Houghton, sneaking behind buildings and keeping an eye out for anyone who might find a man-beast out of the ordinary. Eito snuck around behind the alehouse and checked out the scene. Brock Brunschweiger was out front lifting weights in an effort to impress the local saloon girls while John Hayes sipped his ale and checked his watch chain.

"Where is this Elchick fella?" said Hayes. "He's already two minutes late."

"Kind of a stickler for punctuality aren't you?" asked Brock.

"And you better be too, if you're going to be my minion up at that mine, assuming you beat the crap out of this guy."

"Oh I'm going to beat the crap of him," said Brock. "Lots of crap."

Just then the bartender stepped outside. "When is this fight?" he asked.

"As soon as that coward shows up," said Brock.

"He's already three-and-one-half minutes late," said Hayes.

The bartender looked over at Brock.

"Who's the ball-buster with the watch chain?" he said.

"That's John Hayes, my soon-to-be boss."

"Good luck with that," said the bartender.

"That's enough lip," said Hayes. "If I hear any more out of you, barkeep, I'll buy this whole bar and have you fired."

"But it's *my* place."

"Uh, well what if I offered you two hundred dollars for it?"

"Two hundred?" The bartender looked back over at Brock. "Ball-buster *and* a tight-wad," he said, "Let me know how that job goes."

Just then Eito jumped out of the alley and stood boldly in front of the group in full werewolf glory.

"It's hammer time, Brunschweiger. I'm gonna' rip your throat out!"

Eito's eyes were blood red, his teeth were long and pointed and his claws sharp and ready for thrashing. The hairs on his face stood on end.

"Whoa," said the bartender, "Now *that's* a five 'o clock shadow!"

"What's this?" said Brunschweiger. "You fight in your little wolfie pajamas?"

"I'm going to eat your arms off!" said Eito.

And then it happened. Eito gnashed and thrashed like a wild beast, slashing through Brunschweiger like he was a German-style pork liverwurst stuffed in a natural skin casing. His arms, legs and body were torn to pieces. Brunschweiger was all over the place.

"Uh, I think you won," said the bartender.

"Wow," said Hayes. "I thought you were just going to fight him. I never expected you to dismember and kill him! I love an employee who goes the extra mile—you're hired!"

"You're on!" said Eito.

Hayes addressed the crowd that had formed.

With powers like that we could pull tons of copper out of the ground. Anyone else with supernatural powers is welcome to work for me, but the minion job is taken, right Eito?"

Eito smiled. "I'll see you Monday morning, oooowwweeeooo!"

"That's some howl," said Hayes. "You're not going to do that around the office are you?"

"Do you see that moon up there?" asked Eito.

When Hayes looked up, Eito swooped in and chugged the rest of his beer. By the time Hayes looked back down, Eito was gone.

Eito crept through the hills smiling and thinking about all of the miners he could devour in the U.P. He would never to have to pay for beer again.

He returned to the bush where he had left Mary. Nothing. Mary was gone. Then there was a shriek behind him. Eito turned around and a fuzzy female werewolf jumped on him.

"Whoa, Mary! It's me Eito!"

"I know, you devil, I just can't get enough."

Eito and Mary made sweet werewolf love. Later, the two werewolves purred and smoked cigarettes. Some clouds moved in, blocking the moon and the two lycanthropes changed back into people. They lay there staring up at the nighttime clouds.

"Mary?"

"Yes, Eito."

"I sure hope the moon comes back out."

"Why is that, Eito?"

"Because you're only a six or seven, but as a werewolf, you're like a nine."

"You're no Jack Nicholson."

"Good point."

Mary and Eito hit the road like Bonnie and Clyde. They spent the entire weekend traveling the U.P. on horseback, eating people at night and drinking their ale in the day. At a logging camp in Tequomenon, they ate thirty-three people. They returned to Houghton Monday morning so Eito could start his new minion job at the mine.

Eito entered Hayes' office with a bright, optimistic look on his face.

"Get the hell out of here!" said Hayes.

"What? I'm ready to start my minion job."

"Last time I saw you, you stole the ale from my mug, cost me almost a tenth of a penny! You'll never work in this town again!"

Eito was so enraged he turned into a werewolf. *Wow!* I didn't know I could do it at will, he thought. Eito ripped off parts of Hayes body as Hayes fell to the floor unconscious. Eito tied him up in the office then went outside to the balcony to address the miners over the loud speaker.

(click) "Listen up," said Eito. "I'm Eito Elchick, John Hayes' minion. From now on you'll listen to me. There are eight hundred and forty of you. I want you all to take it easy and not work so hard. I want you all nice and tender. That is all." (click)

When Eito returned to the office, the ropes were on the floor and Hayes was gone.

"Oh well," said Eito, "We'll never see *him* again."

Weeks went by. Eito and Mary lived in Hayes' mansion, eating as many miners as they could. They packed on seventy or eighty pounds a piece. When there were only thirty-two miners left out of eight hundred and forty, several of the miners became suspicious.

"How come there are only thirty-two of us?" asked one.

"Yeah. Why won't they let us do any labor?"

"My brother says that Eito Elchick is a werewolf and he and his girlfriend killed John Hayes and are eating the workers. They're living over at Hayes' mansion."

"They're fat too!" said a worker. "From all of the people they ate!"

Then one of the workers stood up and shouted, "Let's have a twelve-step intervention for them!"

Silence.

Another one yelled, "How about an angry mob!"

"Hooray!" yelled the workers.

"Grab up some torches and pick-axes! We're going over to that mansion!"

The angry mob stormed over to Hayes' mansion, waving torches, pick axes and clubs. Upstairs in the mansion, Eito looked out the bedroom window.

"Uh-oh."

"What is it?" asked Mary.

"Angry mob. We better get out of here."

"Why don't we just kill them?" asked Mary.

"Can't—something about the torches. Man I *hate* angry mobs."

Mary eased out of bed, her fat body impeding her movement.

"Eito, do I look fat to you?"

"Oh yeah, you're huge," said Eito without turning around. "We're both just way overweight."

Mary joined Eito at the window with a beer in her hand. Eito pointed to one of the people in the angry mob. "Hey," he said. "I thought we ate that guy already."

"Yeah I remember him," said Mary. "Maybe it was his brother."

Suddenly something shrieked and jumped out of the bushes. It was a giant werewolf. It started thrashing through the angry mob, killing one worker after another. The speed and force of the angry beast rendered every pickaxe and torch useless. Then Eito noticed that the werewolf was dressed in a tuxedo.

"It's Hayes!" yelled Eito, "And he's dressed for dinner!"

"I thought you said you killed him," said Mary.

"I say a lot of things. Look at his tuxedo."

"Why, so you can steal a sip of my beer?"

"You're not as fun as you used to be."

Hayes continued thrashing through the crowd.

"Well he sure is ripping through that angry mob," said Mary. "How come *you* can't do that, Eito?"

Eito started to worry.

"Yeah, uh, we better get out of here.

They snuck downstairs and made their way to the back of the mansion, moving as fast as their heavy, meat-stuffed frames would allow them. They worked their way down the servant's access and out into the back courtyard. A giant claw came out of nowhere and knocked Mary across the courtyard. She lay dead in the corner.

"Hayes!" yelled Eito. "How'd you kill that angry mob?"

"Angry mobs are communists! My capitalistic werewolf ass hates them! Kill me with my own pickaxes? Not a chance!"

"Holy crap, Hayes, you're super strong!"

"Early to bed early to rise, youngster!"

"And well dressed, too!"

"You stole my mansion, Eito! You stole my mine, and you cost me a tenth of a penny on that beer you stole outside the alehouse!"

"You're still sweating that beer? What about all of the workers I killed?"

"Who cares about them? I own the mortgages on their houses. I'll foreclose, then resell the houses to new workers. This time I'll hire a thousand workers, eight hundred and forty for the mine and one hundred and sixty to eat. Then I can be fat like you, Eito."

"You wouldn't happen to still need a minion, would you?"

"No but I need some onions and gravy 'cause dinner is served!"

Time stood still for Eito. He had to look inside himself. He had to find the strength to defeat Hayes. Mary was dead, all two hundred plus pounds of her. Eito was over three hundred pounds himself. He wasn't sure he could do it, but he had to. He picked up a nearby shovel and swung at Hayes as hard as he could. Nothing but air. Hayes reared up and instantly sliced off Eito's left hand, then his arms, legs and head until he was just a pile of debris. Hayes roared at the moon, bloody and victorious.

"Oooooeeeewwwwoooo!"

But just as Hayes relaxed, something jumped on his head.

"Arrgghhh!" said Mary. "You killed Eito and now I'm gonna make wolf-meat out of you."

"I guess you weren't dead, just unconscious."

"The fake ending," said Mary, "Works every time!"

"Man are you fat," said Hayes as he tried to spin her off of his head, but Mary began singing.

"Whoa," said Hayes. "The fat lady is singing, the fat lady is singing."

Mary went into a rendition of *I Gotta Be Me*, by Ethel Murmon as Hayes screamed for his life.

"Ahhhhhh!"

Then Hayes remembered the advice of his father, a wrestler. He told him that if he ever had a singing fat-lady werewolf on his head, just drop and do a suplex. Hayes did so and Mary flew off to the side. Hayes gathered all of his strength and ripped out Mary's fat throat in a horrible, grotesque manner.

Afterward, Hayes rested on his knees, his tuxedo stained with the blood of Mary, Eito, and the angry mob. He howled at the moon and stood up. "Now where's that mortgage paperwork?" he said.

Hayes disappeared into the mansion. Over in the corner, where Mary had been knocked out, was a little fuzzy fur ball that may or may have not have been a little Eito, leaving us to ask the question—*is this really the end or will there be another ending—again?*

THE END

Coming soon!

Son of Eito—No End In Sight

Also:

The End Again—*Endgame!*

BOOKS BY DALE R. HOFFMAN

YOO PEE FUNNY: A COMIC'S EYE-VIEW OF MICHIGAN'S UPPER PENINSULA

Comedian Dale Hoffman cracks wise on the Upper Peninsula of Michigan in this hysterical collection of previously published articles. Sex, love, hunting, and rural life top the list of laughs in a book that will have you reading aloud to your friends.

ABOUT THE AUTHOR

Dale R. Hoffman is a professional comedian and writer. He lives, farms, and hunts with his wife in Michigan's Western U.P. He is available at drumcomic@drumcomic.com

For more information, visit Dale's website at: http://www.drumcomic.com

CPSIA information can be obtained at www.ICGtesting.com
Printed in the USA
BVOW021349200613

323849BV00003B/5/P